When All Else Fails

Sherryl D. Hancock

Copyright © Sherryl D. Hancock 2020

All rights reserved. No part of this publication may be reproduced, stored in or introduced into a retrieval system or transmitted in any form or by any means, electronic, mechanical, photocopying, recording or otherwise without prior written permission from the publisher.

This is a work of fiction. Names, characters, places and incidents are either the product of the author's imagination or are used fictitiously, and any resemblance to any person or persons, living or dead, events or locales is entirely coincidental.

Published by Vulpine Press in the United Kingdom in 2020

ISBN: 978-1-83919-089-6

Cover by Claire Wood
Cover photo credit: Tirzah D. Hancock

www.vulpine-press.com

For the first responders everywhere!
To the people that show up first in a disaster and risk their lives every day, thank you for your dedication and service!

Also in the WeHo series:

When Love Wins
When Angels Fall
Break in the Storm
Turning Tables
Marking Time
Jet Blue
Water Under the Bridge
Vendetta
Gray Skies
Everything to Everyone
Lightning Strykes
In Plain Sight
Quid Pro Qup
For the Telling
Between Heaven and Hell
Taking Chances
Darkness Past
Stonewall Pride (special anniversary edition)

Prologue

They were pinned down and running out of time. The insurgents were coming in from all sides—they needed a way out! They'd already sustained casualties, and it was just going to get worse. The commander looked over at his lieutenant and shook his head. He wasn't sure there was a way out this time, and he was damned if he was going to die backed into a corner like this.

Suddenly there was the buzz of rotors above them, and the commander saw the most beautiful sight he'd ever seen. An Apache helicopter lowered to hover five feet off the ground, firing into the enemy and taking fire like crazy as the insurgents recognized the bigger threat. The helicopter provided the cover they needed to get out of the corner they'd been backed into.

"Fall back!" the commander yelled to his men, gesturing to the left, where the Apache was covering.

As they watched, the Apache pilot wove the aircraft back and forth, spraying the enemy with cover fire, as a Hellfire missile let go to destroy the tank coming up from the south. The Apache gunner cleared a path that gave the soldiers an escape route, firing continuously even though the helicopter was being hammered by gunfire. A second Hellfire took off, blowing up a truck and a number of insurgents in the process. The helicopter banked right, firing at the group of insurgents who were turning to shoot at the soldiers heading away.

As the last of the insurgents took fire from the Apache, there was a mighty blast—a rocket launcher finally took out the main rotor of the

Apache. The Apache gunner got off one more Hellfire, blowing the truck and the holder of the rocket launcher apart. The Apache banked, its rotor smoking; it went down hard in a dune a click away.

The commander ordered the able-bodied of his men to head for the crash. He really hadn't needed to order it; the men were already running for the crash site. Whoever this pilot and gunner were, they'd just saved their collective asses. The last thing the men were going to do was let them die if the two were still alive.

At the crash, they saw that the Apache was on its side. Men climbed up onto it, throwing open the windows to help the pilot and gunner out of the craft. A shock ran through the men as they realized that both the pilot and the gunner were women. They were hurt, having sustained injuries taking gunfire and in the crash. The gunner had taken a round in the side and had sustained a head wound. The pilot had taken a round in the shoulder and one in the side, and had a head wound as well.

After the medic had done what little he could, they called in an air evacuation for the injured men and the Apache pilot and gunner.

"Jock, you still alive?" the brunette asked.

"Yeah, Gun. You?" replied the redhead.

"Bikini season is definitely over."

"You wear bikinis?"

"No, but if I did, it would definitely be over."

"Captain McGinnis?" a man asked from the foot of the redhead's bed.

"Yeah?" Gage McGinnis lifted her head off the pillow long enough to note that it was a colonel querying. "Sir," she added, almost an afterthought.

Colonel Roberts stepped over to the side of Gage's bed, looking down at her, then over at Jocelyn. "First Lieutenant Mann?"

"Yo," *Jocelyn said, holding up a hand in response.*

"Those were my men you saved yesterday," the colonel said, his tone somber. "That was some serious hero shit."

"We heard the radio call. We were the closest air support," Gage said.

"Yeah, but you didn't have to put your helo in front of the enemy. You could have done it from the air," the colonel said.

"They were closing in on you—there was no time," Gage said. "I knew the sight of an Apache would scare the shit out of them."

"It was the most beautiful thing I've ever seen," the colonel said.

Gage sighed. "She did her job."

"I want you both to know that you saved sixty-nine lives."

Gage and Jocelyn grinned at each other. They'd had the discussion in the copter about what they were willing to do. As always, they were in full agreement.

"Balls to the wall!"

Which was what they'd done. Even when they were taking heavy fire, both Gage and Jocelyn had remained calm and cool. They made a great team; they always had.

Gage and Jocelyn had been a team for the seven years they'd been in the Middle East. They'd been friends with benefits since a month after meeting. It was hard enough to meet women who were gay in the military, but to find one that also wasn't hung up on being in a relationship was even harder. When they'd clicked as friends, the sex had come naturally. If people in their unit suspected their relationship, no one said anything. They were friends; it covered a multitude of sins. Of course, the fact that Gage was married to another Army soldier helped too. They had a kid together—that pretty much proved to everyone that she was straight—and if Gage was straight, her friend Jocelyn was too, right?

Most people considered Gage McGinnis far too hot to be a lesbian anyway, with her long red hair and sultry green eyes. She had a beautiful sweetheart-shaped face with smooth tanned skin, and a sexy set of lips that made most men sigh. Her body was just curvy enough to keep her from being too slim, and she was slightly taller than average at five foot seven. She worked out tirelessly to keep her strength and stamina up, but not so much that it got rid of her curves.

Jocelyn was more butch, with dark brown hair that she wore long and shaggy, and a face that was angular and sharp. She was still quite attractive, with dark eyes framed with long lashes. She was hot in a lanky cowgirl kind of way. She had a long, lean frame, standing five foot ten, taller in the cowboy boots she favored when not in uniform.

"Jock" and "Gun," as they were referred to by their unit, made an interesting team. They were forever laughing, joking and teasing each other. They got along well with their unit members, and everyone liked them. It surprised no one that they'd put themselves in harm's way to rescue fellow soldiers. That was who they were.

It also surprised no one when both women were nominated for and received both the Distinguished Flying Cross and the Distinguished Service Cross for their heroism. They deserved it.

Chapter 1

"Jesus, I'm going to miss this," Gage said as Jocelyn moved to lie at her side, both of them breathing heavily.

"Mm-hmm," Jocelyn said, smiling. "You thought some new fancy job was a great idea two weeks ago.…"

"Wind your neck in there, girlie," Gage said, sounding every bit the Irishwoman that her ancestors were. "I didn't ask for this appointment. Midnight pretty much insisted. You don't tell the new governor for the state of California 'no' if you want to have a future in her state."

"Well, why couldn't you tell her you wanted to be the director for the Office of Emergency Services from San Francisco, instead of insisting on the Los Alamitos office?"

"You know why—I want to be down here with Mark right now, considering… and my family is down here. Hell, I did my ten years up there with you. You should have to do ten with me in LA."

"Ah, hell no. I hate LA," Jocelyn said.

"I wasn't real fond of San Francisco when I got there either," Gage said, narrowing her green eyes.

"Yeah, but since Mark was in San Francisco then, you wanted to be where he was."

"I know," Gage said. "And now that he's down here with a pregnant girlfriend, I need to be here with him."

Jocelyn nodded. "I know the reasons. You just didn't think about this part, that's all," she said, sliding her hand over Gage's stomach.

"Okay, knock it off," Gage said, smiling as she shuddered slightly. "I gotta get up and take you to the airport, and then get my ass to my new job."

"Who'da thought?" Jocelyn said, watching Gage as she got up and stretched, "that you'd end up some high-up mucky-muck?"

Gage turned her head, the red hair that came to two inches past her shoulders falling forward. "Is that what I am?" she asked with a smirk.

"In my head," Jocelyn said, sitting up.

"Fuck…" Gage breathed, sitting back down on the bed next to her best friend. "What if I'm not cut out for this, Jos?"

Jocelyn put her arm around Gage and pulled her over to kiss her head. "You can do anything, Jock. I know that, and you should know that by now. Go kick ass and take names like you always do."

Gage took a deep breath, and her moment of insecurity passed. She got up and took a shower.

An hour later, she was dressed in suit pants and a white collared shirt. She then added her butch flair to it by wearing a set of onyx dog tags around her neck and a thick black rubber-banded aviator's watch on her wrist. Jocelyn happened to know it was a six-thousand-dollar Breitling Cockpit watch, something most people wouldn't know. Gage topped off the outfit with a black leather aviator jacket with a black sheepskin collar. On her feet she wore her usual black combat-style boots; this set had a two-inch heel on them, but still fairly butch-looking. Her hair was back in a ponytail. She wore no makeup, but she still looked pretty damned hot.

"Nice," Jocelyn said, nodding in approval.

"Uh-huh," Gage said, giving Jocelyn a narrowed look. "You got everything?"

"Yeah."

"Okay, then, let's go," Gage said, proceeding out the door of the master bedroom.

Jocelyn took one long last look around and glanced out at the view. The house they were in was a thirteen-thousand-square-foot home in the Hollywood Hills. Gage happened to be the daughter of a very famous old rock star, Lenna McGinnis, who owned the house. When Gage had informed her mother that she was moving to Los Angeles, Lenna had insisted that Gage "just stay at the house." Even Jocelyn hadn't realized how much money her best friend came from until Gage had driven up to the house four days before. The girl didn't brag much, that was for sure.

They were just about at LAX when Gage's department-issued cell phone rang. She rolled her eyes as Jocelyn started grinning.

Hitting the hands-free on the steering wheel, Gage answered the call. "McGinnis."

"Director?" queried a woman's voice.

"Sure, let's go with that," Gage said with a smile.

There was a soft laugh on the other end of line, and Gage and Jocelyn glanced at each other. Jocelyn raised an eyebrow, making a face. Gage just shook her head at her friend's expression.

"Yes, ma'am," the woman said. "This is Kit Landry. Your assistant is out this morning, but I was asked to contact you to let you know there's been a mudslide in Sierra Madre. Forty homes are threatened at this time."

"And let me guess, they want me there?" Gage asked.

"Yes, ma'am," Kit said.

"Do I have air support?"

"Ma'am?"

"Do I need to drive there, or can I catch a ride? If someone has a spare helicopter, I can fly myself," Gage said, grinning.

"I-I..." Kit stammered. "Well, ma'am, I can certainly arrange a helicopter. What airport is closest to you?"

"I'm about five minutes away from LAX, as it happens. Got any LAPD in the area?"

"I'm on it, ma'am," Kit said. "I'll text you the details as soon as I have them."

"Thank you, Kit," Gage said, smiling.

She hung up and looked over at Jocelyn. "Damn, I was hoping to get ahold of a copter."

"Maybe you should get Midnight to give you one," Jocelyn said with a wink.

"Looks like I'm comin' in with ya," Gage said as she went to park her vehicle.

Four hours later, at nearly noon, Gage drove up to the building her offices were located in. She'd had a few text conversations with Kit during the morning. As she pulled into a parking space marked "Director," she saw a young woman with short sandy-brown hair and a kind of soft-butch tomboy look about her standing next to the space and looking at her expectantly.

Kit Landry was surprised by the large black SUV that pulled into the space. It was an Escalade, she knew that by the Cadillac symbol on the grille, but not only was the body of the vehicle black, so was everything else. It was a big, imposing vehicle. The woman that climbed out of it did seem to fit it, however. She appeared every bit as tough and imposing as the vehicle did. Then she smiled.

"You've got to be Kit," Gage said.

"Yes, ma'am." Kit smiled as she handed Gage the binder she was holding.

"Don't call me 'ma'am,'" Gage said.

"Okay, Director."

"Call me Gage," Gage told her. "I'm not big on titles," she said by way of explanation.

"Yes, ma—I mean, okay, Gage," Kit said, grinning.

"Good girl," Gage said. "Now, what am I looking at? And where the hell is the coffee in this place? And I do not need those questions answered in that order."

Kit laughed. The woman was definitely not stuffy, and she was actually pretty funny. She almost envied Molly Xiong, the previous director's secretary. She just didn't know how Director McGinnis was going to handle the girl, since Molly really didn't speak English very well. The previous director had preferred Asian assistants for whatever reason, although as far as anyone knew, he didn't know a word of any language other than English. It had seemed rather bizarre.

Twenty minutes and a large cup of coffee later, Gage was in her office, looking around.

"This is all for me?" she asked. The corner office seemed far too big for one person. "I'm gonna get lost in here."

Kit chuckled. "I can make you a map," she said helpfully.

"Good, you're quick," Gage said, winking at the girl. "Why aren't you my assistant?"

"Well, Molly was the previous director's assistant, and I'm technically only an office tech, so…" Kit trailed off; she didn't want to carry tales.

Gage sensed there was more to the story there, but she didn't want to get into it right then. "Do you have my schedule for the morning?"

"I do—it's in that binder," Kit said, gesturing to the binder Gage had just set down. "First page, under the 'schedule' tab."

"There's a tab and everything," Gage muttered with a smirk. "Is this your work or the other girl's?"

"Mine, ma'am," Kit said. "I mean Gage, sorry. When I got here they told me Molly wasn't going to be in. I couldn't find anything on her desk that... well, that looked like English, so I figured I'd better print out your stuff for you."

"You couldn't find anything that looked like English?" Gage asked, blinking rapidly. "What language was it in?"

"I believe Molly is Chinese, so I'm assuming that's what it was."

"Did the previous director speak Chinese?"

"Not to my knowledge," Kit said.

"Molly speaks English though, right? She maybe just writes in Chinese?" Gage asked hopefully.

"Well, she does speak *some* English, ma'am."

Gage rolled her eyes. "Well, English and some Arabic, mostly cuss words, are all I speak, so this could be a bit of a problem."

"Yes, ma'am," Kit said, looking contrite.

"I'm not blaming you," Gage said, "but what kind of pinhead hires someone that doesn't speak English when they don't speak the language the new employee speaks?"

"The previous director?" Kit said tentatively.

Gage laughed out loud at the look on Kit's face, somewhere between doleful and cheeky.

"So where do I find the classification structure for this place?" Gage asked.

"I can print you out a copy of the organizational chart if that will help, ma'am."

"That's three 'ma'ams' in like five minutes. Don't make me start charging you for them," Gage told the younger girl with a grin.

Kit pressed her lips together, her blue eyes sparkling. She really liked the new director. She seemed like a totally cool person, and definitely someone she'd like to work for.

By the end of her first day, Gage had met with all of her deputy directors and various chiefs of certain sections. There were definitely a few people she wanted to replace. One of her biggest problems was that her second in command had resigned a month before, so she had one huge vacancy.

"Kit?" Gage asked from her office. Kit had taken up the post at the desk right outside.

"Yes, ma—Gage." Kit caught herself as she walked into Gage's office.

"Can you figure out how to get ahold of the governor for me?"

"Of course," Kit said, going back to her desk.

Five minutes later, Kit called, "I've got Governor Chevalier."

"Damn, she's good," Gage said. Even her own secretary at the PD hadn't been this efficient. "Okay, put her through. Thanks, Kit!"

"Good evening, Governor," Gage said, picking up the line.

"Midnight, Gage, Midnight," Midnight said, leaning back in her chair, her booted foot already up on her new desk.

"Got it," Gage said, grinning. "I'm having the same problem with getting my assistant to call me Gage."

Midnight chuckled. "The struggle is real."

Gage chuckled as well. "Look, so I have a few questions…"

"Shoot."

"So, I got no co-pilot here," Gage said. "What am I allowed to do?"

"You can put out a notice for a career executive assignment," Midnight said. "You'll get applications, and then you appoint someone. Do you have anyone in mind?"

"I do, but she'd kick my ass for even asking."

"I had one of those," Midnight said, thinking of Joe Sinclair, the man who had been her second in command when she'd started her gang task force. He'd refused to be her assistant chief when she'd made chief at San Diego PD. "Any backup ideas?"

"Not yet," Gage said, sounding a bit forlorn. "And what about these other deputy directors? Can I replace them if I end up wanting to?"

"Yeah, those are CEAs too, so you can, but make sure you don't get rid of everyone who knows that agency," Midnight said, grinning.

"I try not to be that stupid on purpose," Gage said.

Midnight laughed out loud at that one. She liked Gage McGinnis—the woman was smart and on her game. Midnight knew she was taking a chance in putting her in charge of the Office of Emergency Services, but she felt that Gage's law enforcement background, plus her being a natural leader, would do wonders for an office that had been led by a fairly ineffectual person for years. Gage McGinnis was a mover and a shaker, and Midnight felt that she'd rejuvenate OES for the better.

"So can I make a suggestion?" Midnight asked.

"Of course," Gage said.

"There's a group I want you to meet. They hang out at the Club in West Hollywood," Midnight said. "You may know of some of them through your mom, or through your law enforcement connections. But trust me when I tell you that they're your kind of people."

Gage narrowed her eyes. "Because they're gay?" she asked, knowing that West Hollywood was the gay area of LA, and also knowing about the Club.

Midnight smiled. "You know one of my bodyguards is gay, right? And I don't have a problem with her—she's one of my best friends—

so no, that's not it at all. When I say 'your kind of people,' Gage, I mean that a lot of them are former or current military, and/or law enforcement. In fact, two of them are pilots—one's even a former Black Hawk pilot."

"Really…" Gage said, sounding interested now. "Sorry for the assumption."

"Don't worry about it," Midnight said. "Happens all the time. I guess my being straight makes me seem oblivious to the other half of the world."

Gage grinned, liking that Midnight Chevalier referred to the gay community as the other "half" of the world. It showed that she felt that being gay was perfectly normal.

"Anyway, get in touch with my DLE director, Jericho Tehrani, over in the LA office. I'm sure she can get you introduced to the rest of the girls and Sebastian."

"Sebastian?" Gage queried.

"He's the honorary exception to the lesbians-only rule in the group," Midnight said, chuckling. "Ex-Army Ranger whose best friend is an ex-Marine and one of the supervisors over Covert Ops and Informant Development."

"You weren't kidding with the ex-military, huh?"

"Nope," Midnight said, chuckling. "You might even look at poaching some of Jericho's people, but don't tell her I said that or she'll probably kill me."

"Good to know," Gage said. "I'll get in touch with her."

"Do that, and if you need any help, let me know. I know you can get this agency back in shape, Gage. Just trust your instincts."

"Thanks, Midnight," Gage said, smiling at her end.

They hung up, and Gage called out to Kit again.

"Can you get ahold of Jericho Tehrani? She's the director of the Division of Law Enforcement at DOJ. Last request, I promise!" Gage said.

Kit laughed to herself, shaking her head. Gage McGinnis certainly didn't take her high rank too seriously.

"Happy to do it, Gage," Kit called back as she pulled up the information on the computer. She dialed the number she had for Jericho Tehrani and got her secretary, who put her through once she identified herself.

"I have Jericho Tehrani," Kit called to Gage.

"Give yourself a raise, will ya?" Gage called back. "Then put her through. Thank you!"

"Director Tehrani, this is Gage McGinnis over here at OES," Gage said as she picked up the line.

"Call me Jericho," the DLE director told her.

"Then call me Gage," Gage replied. "I was told by Midnight Chevalier that I should get in touch with you to make some kind of introduction to your group..." Gage let her voice trail off as she realized she wasn't even sure if she knew what she was asking for.

"Yeah, Midnight told me she was going to suggest that," Jericho said, grinning at her end. "She thought you might want a bit of a support network since you're coming from the north."

"Ah, so she warned ya, huh?"

Jericho laughed. "Midnight's good like that. She never leaves a girl hanging."

"Well, she did blindside me with this appointment, so... I am a bit out of my element here," Gage said honestly.

"You free Friday night?" Jericho asked as she checked her own calendar to make sure she and Zoey were available.

"Sure," Gage said.

"You know where the Club is in WeHo?"

"I'm sure I can find it. Haven't been in the scene here in, oh, about twenty-eight years, give or take," Gage said, chuckling.

"I can text you the address, but it's not hard to find. The girls hang out there most Friday nights. I'm sure I can speak for most of them when I say they'd love to meet you."

"I'll be there, then," Gage said.

"Would you want to meet my wife and me for dinner ahead of time?"

"Sure, where?"

"Laurel Hardware, on Route Two?" Jericho suggested.

"Haven't been there," Gage said. "Always up for something new."

"Let's say eight?"

"I'll see you then," Gage said. "Thanks."

"You got it," Jericho said. "We Midnight appointments gotta stick together."

"Amen to that, sister!" Gage said, laughing now.

It was 6 p.m. before Gage stood up from her desk, stretching and reaching into her desk drawer for the holstered pistol she'd placed there when she'd come back from her last meeting. It had been one of the acquiescences she'd gotten from Midnight before she would take the appointment—that she'd receive a CCW, a concealed carry weapons permit, so she could continue to carry a gun. She didn't know how she'd feel being at work without a gun at her back.

Kit walked into the office as Gage turned around to take her jacket off of its hanger and put it on. When Gage turned around, she saw the odd look Kit was giving her.

"The gun?" Gage asked.

Kit nodded.

"I've carried a gun for a good twenty-four years now," she said, smiling. "Wouldn't know what to do without one on me now."

"Twenty-four years?" Kit asked in surprise.

"Yeah," Gage said. "Since I was twenty-two."

Kit looked more shocked. "You're forty-six?"

Gage laughed out loud at that question. "How old did you think I was?"

Kit didn't answer at first. She shook her head. "I don't know, but not even close to forty-six."

Gage gave another soft laugh. "Well, I appreciate that. I've been told I look young for my age. I guess in Los Angeles that's a major compliment, huh?"

"That it is," Kit said, smiling.

"Why are you still here anyway?" Gage asked as she picked up a few things from her desk that she wanted to read. "You got here long before me this morning."

"I just figured you might need help." Kit seemed hesitant suddenly. "I'm sorry, I didn't ask you about overtime..."

"No, don't worry about that," Gage said. "I just assume you have a life or something."

Kit laughed softly. "Well, I do have a child and husband, so I guess that would be considered a life."

"More than me." Gage held up the reports she'd picked up. "This will be my partner tonight."

"Lonely at the top?" Kit asked, her blue eyes dancing with humor.

"That's what they say," Gage said, rolling her eyes. "Come on, let's get out of here. It's dark already."

When they got downstairs, Gage held the door open for Kit.

"So, is this Molly supposed to be in tomorrow?" Gage asked.

"If she's not sick still."

"Here's hoping," Gage said, winking at Kit. "Thank you for all your help today. I really appreciate it."

"You're welcome," Kit said, smiling.

"See you tomorrow," Gage said with a nod.

Kit nodded too, and they parted ways.

Gage got into her truck, checking emails before she started the vehicle. Mötley Crüe's "Kickstart My Heart" flowed from the speakers as her vehicle connected to the iTunes on her phone. She drove out to the street, glanced left, and saw Kit standing at the bus stop. Gage pulled over, opening her window.

"You aren't seriously waiting for the bus…" Gage said.

It was raining and expected to rain harder in the coming hours.

Kit nodded, not sure why Gage was asking.

"No," Gage said, shaking her head. "Get in."

"What?" Kit asked. "Ma'am, I'm fine," she said when she realized what Gage meant.

Gage blew her breath out, putting the Escalade in park and getting out. She walked around and opened the door to the passenger's side, leaning around to look at Kit.

"Get in," she said again in a no-nonsense tone.

Kit's eyes widened as she complied solely on the command in Gage's voice.

Once Kit was inside, Gage shut the door, got back into the vehicle and put it in drive.

"Okay, where to?" she asked Kit.

"Ma'am—"

"Gage."

"Gage," Kit corrected. "I live all the way in Commerce."

"Well, that's right on the way. I live in Hollywood."

"You do?"

"Well, I'm staying in Hollywood, at my mother's house," Gage said.

"Oh," Kit said. "Still, it's out of your way. The bus is just fine."

"Not at this hour, not in the rain, and not when I'm the one that kept you here so late."

Kit bit her lower lip. Her own boss never cared about any of that. Taking a deep breath, she sighed. "Okay."

"You know I'm the boss, right?" Gage said.

Kit smiled. "Yes, ma'am."

"There's that word again…"

"Well, if you didn't have such a commanding presence, I could probably stop calling you it," Kit blurted out before she thought about it.

The look on her face when she realized what she'd just said out loud was priceless.

Gage laughed. "Tell me how you really feel."

"I think I'd like to resign now," Kit said in a small voice.

"I think I'm not gonna let ya," Gage said, her tone serious as she grinned.

"I don't think that's how that works."

"It is in my world." Gage glanced over at Kit with a lopsided smirk.

The girl was really cute. She looked very young, but also very hip, with her short hair spiked slightly in front but curled over at the edges to soften the look. Her makeup was light but emphasized her blue eyes and fair skin. There was a definite soft-butch style to the way she dressed, but Gage knew that some straight girls were doing the tomboy look these days. Gage guessed that the girl was maybe twenty-two or twenty-three.

"So, boy or a girl?" Gage asked as she got on the freeway.

"Girl. Caitlyn," Kit said, smiling fondly.

"How old?"

"She's four."

"Ah," Gage murmured. "That's a tough age. They're really curious about everything and usually only have Mom and Dad as the outlet for that."

"Oh my God, yeah!" Kit said, laughing. "She asks endless questions and has to touch everything."

Gage laughed too, nodding. "Yep, I remember that with my son."

"You have a son?" Kit asked, surprised.

"Yeah," Gage said. "He's twenty now."

Kit looked a bit perplexed, and Gage knew why. It was pretty well-known that Midnight Chevalier's latest appointment was yet another lesbian. There'd been noise from the right that Midnight was purposely putting lesbians in power positions in the government. As usual, Midnight had ignored it.

Gage glanced over at Kit, waiting to see if the girl would ask the questions that she seemed to want to ask. When she didn't, Gage left the topic alone.

They drove in silence for a while, which started to bug Gage, so she turned the stereo up with the controls on the steering wheel.

"California Dreamin'" by Sia came on. Gage grinned—it was the theme song from the movie *San Andreas*, which had depicted "the big one" of earthquakes.

"This should be OES's theme song," Gage said with a chuckle.

Kit laughed too, having been thinking the same thing.

"Too bad the movie got so much wrong," Gage said, rolling her eyes.

"Wrong?"

"Well, the stuff to do with the helicopter and its capabilities."

"It was wrong?" Kit asked. "I loved that stuff!"

"Well, I'm sorry to tell you that you loved completely fictional aviation hoopla."

"And you know this how?"

"Because I flew copters in the Army."

"You did?" Kit asked, surprised yet again.

"Yeah," Gage said. "I flew an Apache attack helicopter."

"Wow, that's really cool," Kit said, sounding very young.

Gage chuckled. "Not when you crash them, unfortunately."

"You crashed?" Kit looked horrified by the idea.

"Well, I was shot down, so it wasn't exactly my fault," Gage said, grinning. "Of course, I was the dumbass who put myself in their way, so…"

"In their way?" Kit queried.

"The insurgents," Gage said. "They had a platoon pinned down. My gunner and I decided to put ourselves and our rig between them and the bad guys."

"Oh my God. Isn't that really dangerous?" Kit asked, thinking it sounded really crazy.

"Well, it worked," Gage said. "But we took a lot of fire, and they nailed my main rotor with a friggin' rocket launcher. But we got them before they got us," Gage said, sounding every bit the Army pilot at that moment.

"So you saved those other soldiers?"

Gage nodded. "The ones that weren't already hit in the original mess."

"That's pretty brave."

Gage had gotten used to hearing people say that over the years, but she'd never gotten truly comfortable with it.

She shrugged. "It's what you do in a war."

"I imagine it's not what everyone does," Kit said. "If it was, there wouldn't be wars for long."

Gage looked back at the girl, her gaze flickering with surprise, but she simply nodded.

Kit was further impressed by the new director. The woman was not just a pretty face; she apparently had a lot of guts. That night when she Googled Gage McGinnis, she ran across an article from three years before, when Gage was a deputy chief with San Francisco PD. She read about the incident at the AG's office in San Francisco, and how Gage had been at the building to do business when a gunman had entered and started shooting people. Gage had been the one to take the man down by shooting him. She was hailed by Midnight Chevalier as being "one executive with a good head on her shoulders and a lot of guts." Kit understood now why Midnight Chevalier had appointed Gage to the position she had.

After Gage dropped Kit off in what she considered a fairly seedy area of Commerce, she called her son, Mark. He answered on the third ring.

"Hey, Mom."

"Hi, babe, how are things going?" Gage asked, already hearing in her son's voice that he wasn't happy.

"Oh, same old shit."

"Okay, what's goin' on, babe?" Gage asked.

"It's Jenny," he said. "She's telling me now that she's not having the baby, that she's going to have an abortion and then she's leaving LA."

"And she's said she's leaving before, babe," Gage said, sighing. "It's probably hormones. Being pregnant is a major roller coaster in the emotions department."

"Is that going to keep me from killing her?"

Gage laughed. "No, probably not. But the fact that your mother used to be a cop should."

"Hey, yeah, how's the new job going?" Mark asked then.

"First day was today, and it was… let's go with interesting."

"Were people annoying?"

"They had their moments," Gage said.

"Good thing you're not carrying anymore, huh?" Mark said, laughing.

"Oh, but I am," Gage said, a grin on her lips.

"Mom!" Mark exclaimed. "Isn't that illegal?"

Gage laughed. "No, babe, I have a CCW. I'm not crazy."

"Oh, whew, good!" Mark said, sounding relieved. "Is Mom J still here?"

"No, Jos went back to San Francisco this morning," Gage said pointedly.

"Damn," Mark said, grimacing at his end, knowing he'd blown it again. "I'm sorry, Mom. I meant to get over to see her… and you… I suck."

"You're stressed," Gage said. "I get that, but you gotta remember who loves you, okay?"

"I'm really sorry, Mom," Mark said. "Things have just been haywire, you know?"

"I know," Gage said calmly.

"I'll come by soon, okay? Did you get all moved in at G-ma's?"

"Yeah," Gage said. "Jos helped. We got our gym time in, hauling shit up stairs."

Mark chuckled, knowing full well that his mother and Jocelyn were two badass women who didn't need a man's help with anything.

It was part of what he loved about them—they were independent and tough, but still incredibly loving and affectionate.

"How come you and Jos never got together?" Mark asked, something he'd always thought about.

"We tried that, way back when. It didn't work," Gage said. "She and I are too much alike—we'd probably kill each other in a relationship. What we have works."

"I know. But, like, now she's there and you're here." He knew that he was partially to blame for that.

"I can find women, you know," Gage said wryly. "Jos isn't literally my only option."

"I know, I know, Mom, you're totally hot and all…" Mark made a gagging sound.

"Fuck you, kid," Gage said, laughing.

"I know you can get women, Mom. I just think you and Jos make a good couple."

"We make good friends. We make lousy girlfriends—trust me on that one."

"Fine," Mark said, sighing. "You just never seem to bother with finding anything permanent, Mom."

"Aren't I supposed to be the one ragging on you about that?"

Mark laughed. "Yeah, but when have we ever been normal?"

"God's truth on that one, bubba."

"Just go find yourself a nice old lesbian and settle down, will ya?" Mark said.

"Old?" Gage repeated in an insulted tone.

"Well, like your age," Mark said, grinning.

"Which is what? Old?"

"Well, you know you are pushing fifty, Mom…"

"Fuck you! I've got four years till I hit fifty!" Gage exclaimed.

"Uh-huh. Right, Mom, sure," Mark joked.

"Don't make me come over there and kick your ass," Gage told him.

Mark laughed. "I gotta go. She's home."

"Oh good," Gage said. "Love you."

"Love you too, Mom. I'll come see you soon."

"I'll hold you to that."

"Ma'am, yes, ma'am," Mark said, grinning.

Gage drove home and walked into the huge empty house. Mark was right; she really needed to find someone more permanent in her life. That night she had potato chips and a beer for dinner and fell asleep reading reports. Such was the glamorous life of the director of the Governor's Office of Emergency Services.

***

Sitting in Caitlyn's room, Kit held her daughter, who was shaking and terrified. It had been an ugly scene, and Kit could only hope that Caitlyn hadn't heard everything. As she glanced down at her arms, Kit was glad it was winter so she'd have an excuse to wear long sleeves tomorrow at work. Jack was getting worse with his drinking and the way he talked to her. She wasn't sure what to do. Fortunately, his violence was contained to her and not directed at Caitlyn at this point, but Kit wondered if that was only a matter of time. Jack was more and more impatient with their daughter, and it worried Kit endlessly. She did everything she could to keep Caitlyn occupied and quiet when Jack was in one of his moods.

"Let's read a story, okay?" Kit suggested softly.

Caitlyn nodded, pointing to the book she wanted her mother to read. She talked less and less these days, another thing that worried

Kit. She'd begun to regret her decision to marry Jack as he'd begged her. She'd been pregnant and afraid of what would happen to her, but it was still no reason to marry a man who'd been an experiment and a huge mistake that resulted in a pregnancy. Just her luck, Kit had thought then. The first man she ever slept with and she got pregnant.

Chapter 2

Gage stared at the young woman, her brain trying desperately to grasp what the woman had just said and had, at Gage's request, repeated twice.

"I'm sorry," Gage said. "Can you write it down?"

Molly looked anxious, her eyes going wide and tears filling them.

"Okay, never mind," Gage said, catching sight of Kit. "Kit!" she called, startling the girl. "Sorry, can you come here, please?"

Kit walked over and saw Molly shifting her weight back and forth in a kind of mincing step, looking extremely anxious.

"It's okay, Molly," Gage said to the young Asian girl. "I've got it."

Gage turned and walked into her office, beckoning Kit to follow her.

"What do you have?" Kit asked, glancing back toward Molly, who was now sitting down at her desk staring blankly into space.

"Nothing. I've got nothing," Gage said, sitting down behind her desk. "Jesus! How did he get anything done? I can't understand a flipping word she says."

Kit did her best to hide her grin but failed miserably.

"Oh, you think it's funny, do you?" Gage said, her expression inscrutable. "Let's see how funny you think this is."

With that, Gage picked up her phone and dialed a number. "Hi, Sharon? It's Director McGinnis. Can you come to my office, please? Yes, right away, thank you."

Gage sat back and waited, looking over at Kit, whose eyes had become wide like saucers. Gage winked at her to relieve the girl's tension a bit.

Sharon, an older, overweight woman with a paunchy face, came in. She gave Kit a cross glance, then addressed Gage.

"Director, is there a problem?" Sharon glanced again at Kit, assuming she was the problem.

"Yes, there is," Gage said, nodding toward her outer office. "That assistant out there won't do me a lot of good until she learns more than a few phrases in English. In the meantime, I want Kit to act as my assistant."

"B-but, ma'am," Sharon stammered. "Kit's only an office technician…"

"So promote her to whatever she needs to be to be my assistant," Gage said simply.

"But, ma'am, that kind of thing takes time!" Sharon exclaimed. "And she's not qualified."

"I have a bachelor's degree in business," Kit said. "Technically I'm more qualified than Molly is, and I'm on the Staff Services Analyst list, rank 1."

Sharon looked over at Kit sharply. Everyone knew that Sharon had made heaven and earth move for the previous director, helping him do whatever he wanted to do personnel-wise, legal or not. Everyone also knew that, in return for that, he always looked the other way when she ran roughshod over her employees, which she did frequently.

"Make it happen," Gage said, her tone brooking no argument. "I don't care if you have to make it a training and development assignment, or we pay her out of classification pay. According to what I read last night, she's qualified to be at the very least an SSA, level D.

So do whatever you need to do to make that happen, and I want it done in the next two weeks. Do I make myself clear?" The last was said in a voice that was all cop, and Sharon paled at the sound of it.

"Y-yes, ma'am," Sharon stammered as she backed out of Gage's office, throwing Kit another foul look.

"Think it's funny now?" Gage asked, her smile wry.

"I don't know what to say…" Kit said, shaking her head.

"You can turn the job down if you really don't want it."

"Oh, I want it," Kit said. "I just never thought I'd get an SSA here. How do you know so much about Personnel?" She knew that Gage hadn't been with the state before; she'd been with San Francisco PD.

"I read up on it last night," Gage said, smirking.

"Wow," Kit said.

"See if you can go help Molly settle… elsewhere, will ya? I can't handle any more tears today."

Kit snorted in subdued laughter.

Gage gave her a dirty look, which only made Kit smile wider.

An hour later, Kit settled into the chair in front of Gage's desk with her notepad in hand.

"Okay, so there's some kind of earthquake preparedness conference going on in San Francisco in two weeks. It's a three-day conference, and we'll need to be at it," Gage said. "Are you going to be able to do that?" she asked belatedly.

"Yes, I have family that can help out," Kit said.

And a husband, Gage thought but didn't say. It wasn't her business.

"I need to arrange a meeting with a few department heads, like Forestry and Cal Fire. Wouldn't hurt to get the local PD and FD heads in here too."

"Got it."

"I think that's enough to keep you busy for a while," Gage said, grinning at Kit.

"Is that the goal? To keep me busy?" Kit asked, grinning back.

"Gotta keep ya off the streets," Gage said, widening her eyes dramatically.

Kit stood up and stretched, pushing up the sleeves of her sweater as she did. Gage caught a glimpse of bruises on both arms, but she said nothing.

Later, as Gage walked out of her office, Kit saw that she had headphones draped around her neck. She was plugging them into her phone as she stopped at Kit's new desk.

"Gonna walk the building," she told Kit.

Kit looked back at Gage questioningly.

"It's a thing," Gage told her, giving her a cavalier wink.

With that, Gage put her headphones in her ears and turned on her music. The music was so loud that Kit could hear it coming out of the headphones. Gage, who was dressed much more casually today, wearing jeans, flat combat-style boots, and a black button-up shirt, walked off.

As she walked through the various work areas, Gage looked at names on cubicles, the people in the cubicles, and the contents of the cubicles, her eyes missing nothing. She continued her walk, garnering odd looks from the employees, and she could see discussions going on behind hands and in asides. She grinned, knowing that people wouldn't know what to make of her, but also using it as a tool to rate various parts of the operation at the building. She could see where time was being wasted and where space was being used inefficiently. She could also see what was working well and who was taking their job seriously, and in some cases too seriously. She was also able to gauge overall morale and attitude in the agency.

An hour later she returned to her office, calling Kit in again.

"I need to schedule an all-hands meeting," she told Kit.

"A what?"

"An 'all hands on deck' meeting, basically all staff in the building."

"Okay," Kit said. "I don't think we have a conference room big enough to fit everyone."

"That's fine, 'cause I don't want to have it here. I want to plan something off-site—I'm thinking paintball or something. How many employees do you think are afraid of guns?"

"Uh… would you like me to conduct a survey?" Kit asked.

"Are you serious?" Gage asked.

"I am, sadly," Kit replied.

"Jesus," Gage rolled her eyes. "No, just plan it for me, will ya? We'll think of some kind of fluffy-bunny tree-huggy thing for the straights…" she said, her voice trailing off as she shook her head.

"Fluffy-bunny tree-huggy thing for the straights?" Kit repeated, barely containing her laughter. "Do you want that on the flyer?"

Gage looked back at her for a long moment, then saw the glimmer of humor in her blue eyes. "Smartass. I like that," Gage said, smiling.

"Do you want to do this before or after the conference?" Kit asked.

"You think you can get it in before the conference?" Gage asked in surprise.

"You'd be shocked and appalled at how quickly I can do things."

"Appalled, huh?" Gage asked, sensing a double entendre but not sure she wasn't imagining or hoping for it.

"Completely disgusted," Kit said, smiling.

"Okay, impress me."

Kit nodded. "Can I assume this will be after work hours?"

"No," Gage said. "If I want to make attendance mandatory, I have to hold it during work hours. We're going to call it an off-site morale builder and bill it that way."

"Okay, I should get procurement onboard early on then," Kit said, thinking out loud.

"No, just get me the figure when you have it."

"But, ma—Gage, we need to get procurement involved and get it approved ahead of time…"

"Not if I'm paying for it," Gage said.

"But we have like a hundred employees…" Kit said, her mouth agape.

Gage grinned. "One hundred and two, actually, but yes, I'm aware."

Kit shook her head, still surprised.

"I'll get on this, right now." Kit stood up.

"Perfect."

The rest of the day sped by, and Gage found that once again it was dark by the time she stood up from her desk. She stretched, feeling her shoulder complain painfully; she gasped out loud as a burning pain ran from her shoulder up through her neck.

"What was that?" Kit asked as she walked up to Gage's desk.

"That was my shoulder having a fit," Gage said. "And telling me that I seriously need to mainline some Vicodin."

"What's wrong with your shoulder?" Kit asked as she pulled on her jacket.

"Nothing an extremely talented surgeon and a series of pins and plates wouldn't solve… Oh wait, that didn't solve it either," Gage said. "It's from the crash back in the Middle East."

"Oh," Kit said. "A surgeon, pins and plates?"

"Everything I've tried so far." Gage reached for her jacket and carefully slid it on, wincing as her shoulder lit up again.

"That doesn't look like much fun," Kit said.

"Then I'd advise you not to sign up for a major shoulder injury with a round from an AK-47 in it."

"You were shot too?" Kit asked, her eyes wide.

"All at the same time, actually," Gage said as she escorted Kit out of the office and to the elevators.

"So you were shot and crashed?"

"Twice," Gage said.

"Twice?" Kit asked as she walked into the elevator.

"Shot twice, and crashed."

"Where else were you shot?"

Gage touched her side, just below her right breast. "Here and the shoulder."

"And the shoulder is the one causing the problems," Kit said.

"Because the other round went straight through. The one in my shoulder hit and shattered bone and stayed in there," Gage said. "They probably caused more nerve damage when they took it out than it did going in."

Kit grimaced. "That doesn't sound good."

"Army doctors aren't exactly specialists. They patch you up and ship you back to your unit."

"But don't people usually get discharged when they get hurt like that?"

"You have the option, yeah," Gage said as they walked out of the building. "I didn't take it."

"You stayed in on purpose?" Kit asked, looking dumbfounded.

Gage laughed, nodding her head. "I guess I was a glutton for punishment."

"I guess…" Kit agreed. "Well, good night," she said, turning toward the bus stop.

"Where do you think you're going?" Gage asked.

"Um, home?"

"Truck," Gage said, pointing to her vehicle.

"It's not raining…" Kit said.

"Is it dark?"

"Yes, but—"

"Yes," Gage said, then pointed at her vehicle again. "Truck, now."

"But…"

"You really want to go there?" Gage asked.

"Where?" Kit asked, mystified.

"Wherever you were headed with your 'but,'" Gage said.

"Maybe?" Kit queried, looking less sure by the second.

"No," Gage said, shaking her head. "Truck, now."

"Bossy…" Kit muttered as she turned toward Gage's SUV.

"I am the boss, you know."

"Braggart," Kit muttered then, eliciting a laugh from Gage.

Gage opened the passenger door and waited for Kit to climb inside before getting in on the other side. This time when she turned on the vehicle, a rock song played on the stereo. The stereo said it was the KillSonik remix of Linkin Park's "Lost in the Echo." Kit was surprised when Gage sang the words. Linkin Park was known for its rap-rock style, and the fact that Gage was able to sing the rap portion was surprising. Kit found the lyrics interesting and wondered if the fact that she was so familiar with lyrics that talked about coming back unshaken from difficult times said something more about Gage.

"I like that song," Kit said as it ended.

"Yeah, me too," Gage said. "My son got me into Linkin Park."

"He likes rock, huh?"

"Yeah," Gage said. "And forever trying to get me into different bands. Some hits, some misses."

"You're lucky. I'm still stuck with 'The Wheels on the Bus Go Round and Round,'" Kit said, laughing.

"Ugh, yeah, I remember those days. Fortunately, Mark liked whatever we listened to at the time, so he got into bands like Mötley Crüe and Def Leppard."

"Oh, wow, I'm not sure how that would go over with Caitlyn," Kit said, shaking her head.

"Maybe girls are different," Gage said, grinning.

"Maybe," Kit said. "I always wanted a little girl, so maybe I'm the one forcing crazy stuff like *Frozen* on her."

"Oh, I doubt it," Gage said. "Disney seems to have a corner on that market."

Kit laughed. "Need to buy stock in them."

"I think I have some," Gage said, looking thoughtful for a moment.

"Smart move."

"Thank my mother's accountant," Gage said. "I'd have no clue otherwise."

"I'd just like to make enough money to *have* an accountant," Kit said.

"I actually took a cut in pay to take this job," Gage said with a grin.

"Are you serious?"

"I don't get overtime anymore," Gage said, shrugging.

"Well, that kind of sucks," Kit said.

Gage smiled. "It's supposed to be good for my career."

"Less money is less money," Kit said.

"S'okay. I get my benefits from the military and the additional pay for the cross and all."

"The cross and all?" Kit queried in disbelief. "Would that be the Distinguished Service Cross that you received for your helicopter escapade?"

A slow grin spread across Gage's lips. "And how did you find out about that?"

"I did some research on you, boss," Kit said, smiling. "I also know what you did in San Francisco three years ago."

"Isn't that a movie?" Gage asked.

"That's *I Know What You Did Last Summer*, Gage," Kit said, her tone reflecting her narrowed eyes. "You're like this major hero, boss lady."

"I was in the wrong place at the right time in San Francisco," Gage said.

"And you were a hero and saved a lot of lives."

Gage rolled her eyes.

"Don't do that," Kit said. "You should be extremely proud of yourself."

"I did my job."

"Really? It was your job to take out a gunman in the Attorney General's offices?" Kit asked.

"When you're a peace officer, you're a peace officer all the time," Gage said. "So yeah, technically it was my job to intercede when people's lives were in danger."

Kit gave Gage a measuring look; she could see that Gage honestly believed what she was saying and that she didn't in any way see herself as a "hero."

"That title, 'hero,' really bugs you, doesn't it?" Kit asked.

"Pretty much," Gage said mildly.

"Why?" Kit asked, really curious.

"Because both times the word has been ascribed to me I feel like I was doing the job I was paid to do."

"How much is your life worth?" Kit asked.

"How much is anyone's life worth?" Gage countered.

Kit was finding her boss more and more of an enigma. She'd heard people all over the agency describe the new director with that word, because they couldn't figure her out. That day's walk-through of the office space had only further served to back up the idea that the woman was not your average politician or executive. Kit was seriously beginning to agree with the description, but for other reasons than what the average employee saw. Gage McGinnis was far from average. She seemed to take everything she did seriously, but with a sense of humor and humility about it. Kit could not figure the woman out to save her life, but she found her extremely interesting.

***

Friday night rolled around, and Gage managed to drop Kit off at home and, with traffic, just make it to the restaurant ten minutes early. She ordered a shot of bourbon and a beer at the bar and sat waiting for Jericho and her wife. Looking around her, she decided that the place was definitely interesting. The outside was still apparently the original facade of an old hardware store. The inside had an industrial feel, but it was a nice casual atmosphere. Gage glanced down at her clothes—at least she'd worn jeans that day, since she hadn't had time to go home and change. She also wore an emerald-green tank top with a black jacket, with her favorite combat-style boots and a black leather belt with a silver-and-green Celtic cross buckle. Her hair was pulled back at the top; the rest fell down her back. She figured she was acceptable for a night out—not top of her game, but acceptable.

Jericho located Gage by her red hair; she'd seen her on the news when Midnight had appointed her. The woman was definitely inordinately hot, she'd give her that. Her hand in Zoey's, Jericho walked over to the bar.

"Gage?"

Gage turned around, her green eyes settling on Jericho Tehrani. The woman's eyes were an amazing shade of blue, Gage thought as she moved to stand. She smiled at Jericho and then glanced at Zoey, a beautiful blonde with blue eyes as well. She nodded to Zoey as she extended her hand to Jericho.

"Good to meet you," Gage said.

"You too," Jericho said.

They headed over to the table the hostess was holding for them. Both Jericho and Gage remained standing until Zoey sat down, grinning at each other as they did. It was a butch thing.

"This is an interesting place," Gage said.

"Zoey dragged me here the first time," Jericho said. "I normally wouldn't touch anything this trendy to save my life."

"But she loves the food," Zoey said, giving her wife a knowing look.

"I admit it, it's pretty good," Jericho said.

"I see a cheeseburger, so I figure I'm safe," Gage said, tongue in cheek.

Zoey rolled her eyes. "Oh, God, you're like her."

"Sorry, babe, you know I'm not a foofy food kind of girl," Jericho said, seeming unapologetic about that fact.

"This isn't foofy food," Zoey said. "Sheesh!"

Jericho looked over at Gage. "Help me out here…"

Gage looked at the menu and shrugged. "It's a bit on the fluff side, but I've been to much worse in San Francisco."

"Damn." Jericho shook her head as Zoey smiled triumphantly.

"Sorry," Gage said. "Jos used to drag me somewhere new every other night—she's like this major foodie."

"Jos?" Zoey inquired.

"My best friend," Gage said. "She was my co-pilot in the Army."

"You flew copters, right?" Jericho asked.

"Yeah, I also flew jets. Copters were more fun though."

"I heard something about an Apache?"

Gage put her tongue between her teeth, looking abashed as she nodded.

"Saved a lot of lives, is what I heard," Jericho said with a pointed look.

"What happened?" Zoey asked.

"Apparently Gage here used an Apache helicopter as a shield to protect a platoon of men who were pinned down by insurgents."

Zoey's eyes widened. "I don't know much about helicopters or the military, but isn't that kind of crazy?"

Gage laughed and took a drink of her beer. "It did the trick."

"Got you shot down, too, didn't it?" Jericho asked. "Pretty fuckin' brave."

Gage shrugged, seemingly unimpressed with herself.

Zoey glanced at Jericho as Gage pointedly went back to looking at the menu. Jericho shook her head, rolling her eyes at her wife. Zoey pressed her lips together; Jericho wasn't exactly one to criticize someone who didn't want to be labeled as brave. Jericho had literally charged a man with a knife to protect Zoey, almost getting killed in the process, and would never let anyone call her "brave." Gage and Jericho were two of a kind.

After they ordered, Jericho and Gage got to talking about OES and what Gage's plans were for the agency.

"I need to replace some executive staff. Some have already retired, others are talking about it, and I'm encouraging that," Gage said, grinning.

Jericho nodded. "I get that. I had a lot of excess baggage when I got to DOJ too. What positions are you looking to fill?"

"Well, top of my list is the chief deputy director. I've got an idea on that one, but I'm not sure she'll even consider it. Then I'm looking at replacing the deputy for crisis communications and media relations, my logistics deputy, my CIO and my response deputy."

"What's a response deputy do?" Jericho asked.

"Works closely with Fire and Rescue and law enforcement," Gage said.

"And Midnight wanted you to get in touch with the group, huh?" Jericho asked, her blue eyes narrowed in suspicion.

Gage started laughing. "Hey, I was completely ignorant until she told me that."

Jericho nodded. "I know some people you should talk to, that's for sure. I'd hate like hell to lose them, but it might be a good fit."

"Any suggestions you can make would be greatly appreciated," Gage said. "I'm really wanting to blue the place up a bit, ya know? It's like the place is being run like a corporation and not a response agency. Cops know how to respond."

"Betting that's what Midnight had in mind when she put you in place."

"Pretty much."

Later, at the Club, Jericho introduced Gage to the group, focusing on certain people. The first two women she introduced Gage to were Gray Black Wolf and Skyler Boché, fellow pilots.

"Apache, and Hornets sometimes too," Gage said, smiling at the other two.

"Black Hawk," Skyler said.

"Raptor," Gray said. "And more recently whatever Shen gets me." She winked at Shenin Hancock.

"You get air support?" Gage asked Shenin.

"Yeah, for now I'm the Air Force's air support liaison," Shenin said.

"For now?"

"Yeah," Shenin glanced over at her wife, Tyler. "We're expecting in about six months, so I'm getting out next month."

"Much to our chagrin," Jericho said, grinning. "But happy for them too. Shenin is technically a logistics officer," Jericho said pointedly.

"I see…" Gage said, her look contemplative. "What are your plans for when you discharge?"

Shenin shrugged. "Don't really know yet. Why?"

"Maybe we should talk," Gage said.

"Did I mention that Gage is the new director over the Office of Emergency Services?" Jericho grinned. "And she's here on a poaching mission," she added with a widening of her blue eyes.

"We should definitely talk," Shenin said.

Jericho turned to put her hand on a blond woman. "Now, Gage, this is Kashena Windwalker-Marshal—"

"I know them," Gage said, smiling as she recognized both Kashena and Sebastian and walking over to shake hands with them both.

"Gage was the one to debrief us when she handled an active shooter situation for us in San Francisco," Kashena explained as she shook hands with the other woman.

"I hope you've tightened those boys up since then," Gage said, grinning.

"Trust me, we did," Sebastian said. "A couple of them got a good tuning-up for their lack of response."

Kashena smirked. "Baz enjoyed that part."

"Damned right!" Sebastian said, his expression sour.

"They all got POST certified after that," Kashena told Gage.

"Active shooter incident?" a black-haired woman asked.

"Gage, this is Jet," Jericho said, nodding to the woman who'd just asked the question.

Gage shook hands with Jet. "Yeah, they had a shooter in the building. I neutralized him."

"Permanently," Sebastian said, tapping his forehead.

"Nice," Jet said.

"Jet's former Army too," Jericho said. "She was a military information officer, right?"

"Yep," Jet said.

"And my best in asset development," Kashena added.

Gage looked at Jet—the woman was definitely a stunner with her dark hair and light green eyes.

"This is my wife," Jet said, gesturing to an exotic-looking girl with silver-gray eyes. "Fadiyah."

Gage recognized the girl as being Middle Eastern, so rather than extending her hand, she merely inclined her head with her hand over her heart.

"It is nice to meet you," Fadiyah said with a smile.

"Are Harley and Shiloh coming tonight?" Jericho asked the group.

"I think Harley got back earlier this week." Rayden extended her hand to Gage. "Rayden Black Wolf," she said, smiling.

"Ray's in charge of LA IMPACT as a whole," Jericho said.

Gage smiled, shaking the other woman's hand. "And married to Gray?"

"I like to think of it as she's married to me, but…" Rayden grinned.

"Hey!" Gray laughed as she swatted her wife on the arm.

"Ray's a former Navy Seal," Jericho said.

"Man, Midnight wasn't kidding about a lot of former military, was she?"

"Nope," Jericho said. "There's Remi, Kai and Legend," she said, as she pointed to each of them, "who are former Marines like Kash. Of course, Shen and Tyler are Air Force like Gray was. Jet, Sky, and Baz, former Army like you. Then obviously there's Ray and also Parker who are former Navy."

Gage shook her head. "Big damned group," she said, laughing.

"You have no idea," Kashena said. "Not all of us are even here tonight."

"Yeah, where are Lyric and Savanna?" Kashena asked. "And for that matter Cody and McKenna?"

"They're on vacation," another woman with dark hair said.

"Oh, that's Dakota," Jericho said, pointing to the person that just spoke. "She's with Jazmine, who is as usual out on the floor with Cat, Jovina, Natalia and Raine," Jericho said. "And there's Memphis and Kieran in the DJ booth."

"Sin and River aren't here either," another woman with an Irish accent said. "But I am."

"That's Quinn, and her girlfriend, Xandy," Jericho said, winking at Xandy.

"Xandy Blue…" Gage said, a little shocked.

"She gets that a lot," Quinn said, extending her hand to Gage with a wicked grin.

"Stop it," Xandy said as she extended her hand to Gage as well. "Nice to meet you."

"You might recognize Wynter too," Jericho said, pointing to the woman walking toward the table.

"Holy shit," Gage said, looking a bit starstruck.

"Hold on to your boots," Quinn said as she turned Gage around to point out Riley Taylor and Talon Valois talking at the bar as they waited for drinks.

"Okay, Midnight didn't warn me about that," Gage said.

"Well, I hear tell your mother's kind of famous too," Jericho said.

Gage rolled her eyes. "Yeah, kind of."

"Lenna McGinnis?" Jericho said.

"Seriously?" Quinn said, her face draining of all color.

"Well, that never happens," Xandy said gleefully. "Babe, are you okay?"

"Your mother is Lenna McGinnis?" Quinn asked, still looking shocked.

Gage nodded. "I take it you're a fan."

"She's fecking Irish. Of course I'm a fan!" Quinn exclaimed, causing the entire group to laugh.

No one had ever seen Quinn starstruck before. It was quite amusing to everyone.

Gage laughed. "Well, when she comes back to town I can certainly introduce you."

"You'd be my new best friend," Quinn said.

"Thanks," Jericho said, grinning.

"You'll recover, Jerich," Quinn said, winking at Jericho.

Jericho shook her head in mock sadness. "Dunno."

"I'm staying in her house here in the hills," Gage said. "If you wanted a tour…"

Quinn's eyes widened, and once again everyone laughed.

"Party at Gage's house!" Quinn said.

Gage laughed. "That can be arranged. The damned place is huge."

"How big are we talking?" Kai asked, as she entered the conversation.

"Thirteen thousand," Gage said.

"Holy shit," Kai said, laughing. "Are you there alone?"

"Yeah," Gage said. "It's depressing as fuck."

"Sounds like Quinn'll move in with ya," Legend said.

"Hey!" Xandy exclaimed, smacking Legend on the ass.

"Ohh," Legend said, waggling her eyebrows at Xandy.

"What's going on over here?" Riley asked as she handed Legend a beer.

"Quinn's moving in with Gage, and Xandy's flirting with your wife," Kai said.

"Hey," Riley said, narrowing her eyes at Xandy. "Back off, girlie."

The group had a good laugh at that one. Gage noted that Talon Valois sat down next to the woman Jericho had called Parker. It was definitely a couples situation in this group. Gage felt a little like the odd man out.

"So the important question is, what do you drive?" Quinn asked.

Gage looked around the group and saw expectant faces. "Well, my daily is an Escalade… but I'm betting that's not the real question here, is it?" she asked with a sly grin. "My weekend get-into-trouble car is the Bandit Edition Trans Am."

A big exclamation went up from the group.

"Ohh," Quinn exclaimed. "Serious?"

Gage inclined her head, glad she'd apparently passed that test.

"Nice," Quinn said. "We'll need to race."

"What do you drive?" Gage asked.

"A '70 Charger and a '69 Mach," Quinn said.

Gage was sufficiently impressed. "Name the time and the place, I'll be there."

That was apparently the right thing to say, because the group nodded and grinned.

"The actual important question," said the blonde from the DJ booth, "is what kind of music you listen to."

"This is Memphis," Jericho told Gage. "Her world revolves around music."

Gage smiled. "Well, I listen to a lot of classic rock—Crüe, Leppard, Van Halen. My son got me into Linkin Park, but yeah, mostly rock."

Memphis nodded, narrowing her blue eyes slightly. Gage got the distinct impression she was being evaluated. She looked back at Memphis, a slight smile on her lips, the look in her green eyes direct. After a long moment, Memphis smiled.

"I can work with that," she said.

"Why am I sure I should be afraid right now?" Gage asked, causing a laugh to go through the group.

Quinn winked at her. "Because you have good instincts."

"But can you dance?" asked another woman, a really beautiful dark-haired Latina with a bright smile.

"This is Natalia," Jericho said, "and that's Raine, her fiancée, and Cat and Jovina—oh, and Jazmine over there with Dakota." She pointed to the other women that had come back to the table.

Natalia gave Gage an imperious look. "So? Can you?" she asked in her thick accent.

"Dance?" Gage asked.

"Si, dance," Natalia said, smiling.

"I suppose." Gage saw that everyone was watching the exchange with interest. "Why?"

"Nat teaches a cardio dance class, and most of the girls do it. We butches avoid it like the black plague," Quinn said.

"Because butches can't hack my class," Natalia said, putting a hand on her hip and moving her head around with a sassy attitude.

"Ohh, now that's low," Quinn said caustically.

Natalia shrugged at Quinn, then looked back Gage, who was barely holding back a grin, her eyes dancing in amusement.

"Qué?" Natalia queried. "You have something to say?"

Gage looked back at Natalia as someone handed her a shot. She glanced over at Jet, who gave her a wink. Gage did the shot, then focused back on Natalia.

"I'll bet you I can do your class and only miss a step here or there," Gage said.

Natalia made a noise in the back of her throat. "No way!" she said, shaking her head, as did many of members of the group. "This isn't some easy Zumba class, juera. This is a real workout."

"And I'm betting you I can do it."

"What's the bet for?" Jet asked.

"Let's make it interesting," Jericho said. "If Gage wins, Nat has to buy drinks all night next Friday."

"And if I win?" Nat asked.

"Then the drinks are on Gage," Jericho said.

Gage grinned. "So you all win no matter what."

"You got it," Jericho said, winking at Gage.

"It's a bet," Gage said.

"Si, a bet," Natalia agreed, extending her hand to Gage.

Later in the evening, Gage got an opportunity to meet Harley Davidson. Jericho told her that Harley was a computer genius who was looking to settle into a job, not liking all the traveling she had to do with her current assignment. Gage also met Shiloh, Harley's reason for wanting to be home more. Gage couldn't argue with that; Shiloh was a beauty.

On her way home that night, Gage felt a familiar ache. She'd seen all the couples that night and felt like she was missing something in her life. Most of the time it didn't bother her that she didn't have a life partner. She and Jos had their thing, which had been great when they were in the same city, but even then, it wasn't the real deal. In a way she longed to find love, but in another way she worried about it. She could see with the couples she'd been around that night that sometimes love was an awesome thing, but she'd also seen couples who fought all the time and were unhappy in their relationships. She knew she had to find the right thing for her; she just had no idea what it would look like.

Chapter 3

The morning of the "all-hands" meeting dawned clear and bright and, very fortunately, not too cold for a Wednesday on a February morning. Gage picked Kit up at her apartment. She noted that Kit was outside waiting when she arrived.

"I could have come up," Gage said.

"It's okay," Kit said, smiling as she got into the truck.

Gage gave her a long, assessing look, but finally she nodded and put the truck into gear.

"So we're all set up, right?" Gage asked Kit.

"Yep, it's about twenty-five minutes from the office."

"Perfect," Gage said. "I checked out the website you sent me. It looks friggin' awesome."

"Yeah, I've heard really good things about the place, and we have it for the full four hours."

"And they have that beginners' paintball version, which was genius, Kit. Kind of the fuzzy-bunny option, but for everyone," Gage said, really impressed with her new assistant's work.

"Oh, that was just icing on the cake," Kit said. "The restaurant is about twenty minutes from the park—I've got maps for everyone. And you're still sure you want to pay for everyone?"

Gage nodded. "Can't pay for food with state funds."

"Well, no, but we could expense the park…"

"Nope, I got it," Gage said with a smile.

"You realize that this day could cost you upwards of five thousand dollars between the park and food," Kit said, unable to believe the figure.

"I got it," Gage said earnestly.

"That's more than I make in a month," Kit said.

"Not more than I make in a month."

"Uh-huh…" Kit said, shaking her head.

"Relax, will ya?" Gage grinned. "This is supposed to be a fun day."

Gage was looking forward to it. As soon as the email had gone out about the "team-building off-site," the challenges between programs had started. Fire and Rescue had challenged the Earthquake and Tsunami program, Media had challenged the Rail and Transit Security team, Emergency Services had challenged the Field Operations group—it had gotten to a fun level very quickly. Kit had been amazed at how many people were really excited about the off-site.

There'd been no complaints about the location or the restaurant for lunch afterwards. Kit was actually fairly certain that it was because there was literally no cost to the employees. Kit had gotten a panicked a visit from the administrative services manager, however, freaking out about how it was going to be paid for. When she'd told the manager that Gage was paying for everything, the woman had nearly fainted.

The fact that the director was paying for the entire day out of her own pocket had also spread through the agency like wildfire. Kit noted that employees seemed very grateful to Gage for that, and she wondered if that had been part of Gage's plan all along.

"So is that your paintball outfit?" Kit asked. Gage was wearing Army fatigues, complete with the sand-colored boots.

"Hooah," Gage said, grinning.

"That's an Army thing, right?"

Gage chuckled. "Yep."

Kit looked over at her boss. She was definitely far from the executive type. On this particular day, in addition to her Army battledress uniform, she wore her hair in a long braid down her back, no makeup, no jewelry other than her black dog tag necklace and her watch. The BDU shirt was open to reveal a black V-neck tank top, and the sleeves were efficiently rolled up. She looked sharp in a very military way, which was odd for an office setting, but Kit thought it was likely that Gage had a reason for that as well. It seemed that Gage had a reason for most everything she did.

The staff gathered in one of the more open areas of the park, which had an old out-of-commission helicopter parked in it, one of the many props of the park. Everyone talked excitedly as they waited to hear from the director. Once everyone was gathered, Gage climbed up on the helicopter and sat on the top, her feet dangling where the helicopter's windshield would have been. She gazed out over the group gathered there. Kit had told her that literally every employee that worked for the Riverside office had shown up, which was amazing.

"For any of you who haven't heard, I'm Gage McGinnis, and I've been appointed as the director of this agency," Gage said, her voice loud enough to be heard, but holding no amount of ego whatsoever.

She put her hand down on the roof of the helicopter. "And for those of you who haven't Googled me yet," she said, winking at Kit, "I used to fly Apache helicopters for the Army."

A lot of people clapped or called out in response to that statement.

Gage laughed. "I learned one thing when I was in the Army, and it was that when the shit hits the fan, you gotta be there to do your job."

That was met with cheers and a lot of heads nodding.

"That's what this agency is about," Gage said. "That's our job. We're here because the people of the great state of California need us. It might not happen today, maybe not tomorrow, but when everything is going to hell, we'll be there to help, and we need to be ready to do just that." Her eyes ranged over the staff and then stopped at one. "Bill Cobbs, you have a lot of ideas, don't you?"

The older black man looked surprised to be singled out, but then he nodded. "Yes, ma'am!" he yelled back.

Gage's eyes scanned the group again, stopping at a tall woman with long brown hair. "Teresa Pino, you have ideas too, don't you?"

The woman also appeared shocked to be called out, but nodded her head. "No one has listened to them though."

"Well, that changes today," Gage said. "As of today, I want to hear everyone's ideas on how to make this agency better."

Again, a cheer went up from the employees, but Gage held up her hands.

"Now, don't get me wrong—I won't put everything into practice, and I'm telling you all right now, don't you dare come to me with a problem if you don't have a solution. This is not an invitation for a bitchfest." She knew she was pushing her luck with the cuss words, but she also wanted to get her point across. "It's an invitation to share ideas about the agency and ways to move it forward. I get that there are problems, and I'm more than happy to work on those problems too, but we need to prioritize."

"I am going to set up an intranet email box with a place for suggestions. If your idea warrants a meeting with me, then my assistant, Kit, will make those arrangements and will contact you to do so. Please feel free to send in ideas—again, I'd appreciate it if you can give me workable solutions. I don't expect anyone to solve everything, but I need to know a direction."

Her eyes scanned the group again. "I want this agency to be on its game when the time comes for us to step up to the plate. And I need people working here that are committed to that mission. So, for anyone that just wants to coast, consider this my formal invitation to succeed elsewhere with the State of California." Her smile was wintery.

There was a little bit of foot shuffling, and a lot of nodding and exchanging of looks.

"So, with all that being said, let's have a good time today. Please don't make me do any worker's comp paperwork," she said with a cavalier wink, "but have fun, and enjoy this time with your co-workers. Let the games begin!"

A cheer went up in the crowd, and Gage climbed down off the helicopter. She was met by not only Kit but a few staff who simply wanted to shake her hand.

"Thank you for your service," one woman said, smiling at Gage. "My son is over in Afghanistan right now."

"I know, Ruth," Gage said. "It looks like he's with infantry."

"Y-yes," Ruth said, looking stunned.

Gage smiled. "I saw the pictures in your cubicle. You have every right to be very proud of him."

"I am," Ruth said, seeming even more impressed with the new director.

A man walked up, extending his hand to her even as he gave her a furtive look. "Nice to meet you, Director," he said in tone that was somewhat odd.

"You too, Johnny," Gage said, tilting her head to catch his eyes and smiling up at him. "I understand you're our wonder in the mailroom, keeping everything going where it's supposed to go."

The man looked at Gage, his eyes wide. "Yeah," he said with a smile. "Yeah, I do."

"Well, keep up the good work," Gage said. "And have fun today."

"I will, ma'am!" he said, happy as he walked away.

There were a few other discussions just like the first two, which Kit stood back watching and couldn't believe. When the group had cleared, Gage turned to Kit and saw her expression.

"What?"

"You're gonna have to explain this later," Kit said, gesturing around her to indicate what had just happened.

Gage laughed. "Come on, let's go greet my guests," she said, winking at Kit.

"Guests?"

"Yep," Gage said as she led Kit toward the front of the park, where a small group stood. "Kit, I want you to meet Kashena Windwalker-Marshal, Sebastian Bach, Harley Davidson and Shenin Hancock."

Kit nodded at each person, her eyes slightly wide. She saw that three of them wore badges and guns, and the other was dressed in military fatigues like Gage.

"All I want to know," Kit said, circling her finger to indicate Gage and the rest of the group, "is what team you guys are going to be on, because that's the one I'm picking!"

Gage laughed, as did the others.

"Tighten it up back there, Marine," Sebastian growled.

"Bite my ass, Ranger," Kashena retorted. "You're the one that's moving too fast for the rest of the group."

Sebastian smirked. "Getting out of shape there, Kash?"

"I can still take you any day of the week, and twice on Sunday," Kashena answered.

"Okay, okay, let's keep the chatter down," Gage said. "Shen, move to your right. They're coming up on your flank."

"This is a lot less fun than a computer game," Harley groused, but grinned all the same.

Kashena laughed. "You went to an academy, didn't you?"

"Yeah, but who paid attention to this part?" Harley said.

"All of us," Gage said, deadpan.

"Just the ones that didn't want to get shot on our first day," Sebastian said.

"They taught us this in boot camp a hundred years ago," Shenin replied.

"Oo-rah," Kashena answered.

"Fuckin' Marines," Sebastian said, shaking his head.

Kashena smacked him on the back of the head. "Watch your mouth, Ranger. Kit doesn't want to hear that stuff."

"I hear that stuff from Gage, regularly," Kit put in, laughing.

"Gage! Shame on you!" Harley said. "Didn't you get the manual that says not to cuss in front of the staff?"

"There's a manual that says that?" Sebastian asked.

"It's the common-sense manual. They don't bother giving it to Rangers, 'cause they know you can't read." Kashena's blue eyes danced in amusement.

"If I get hit with a paintball because of you two chuckleheads…" Shenin muttered.

"Chuckleheads?" Kashena and Sebastian said together.

Suddenly there was the sound of paintballs flying. Kashena and Sebastian immediately went on the attack. Harley hung back, glancing over at Gage.

"Are you sure you want to deal with those two on a regular basis?"

Gage looked back at Harley, loving the two thin rainbow-striped braids that hung down her chest, the rest of her white-blond hair up in a messy ponytail.

"Some days I'm not sure," Gage said, grinning.

"We better get in there to back them up," Shenin said. "Or we'll never hear the end of it."

"True that," Harley said.

"Let's go," Gage said, putting her paintball gun up and moving on.

Later at the restaurant, Gage talked to the four quietly before they sat down. Kit was surprised when they each walked over to a different area of the tables to sit down. They'd taken over the entire huge restaurant.

Gage sat down at a small table with Kit. She ordered a beer and sat back, extending her legs in front of her and crossing them at the ankles.

"You got a little…" Gage picked up her napkin and leaned forward to wipe a smudge of paint off Kit's cheek.

"That was your fault, you know," Kit said.

"I know, but it was funny," Gage said, looking unapologetic.

"They shot each other…" Kit said.

"Yeah, they're best friends," Gage said. "My guess is the rivalry goes deep. Just be happy you only got a glancing blow."

"So… what are they really doing here?"

Gage simply looked back at her, her green eyes sparkling.

"The exec spots," Kit said, pursing her lips. "I can see that."

"We'll see," Gage said noncommittally.

After a while, Gage got up and walked around to the various tables, talking to employees and making what Kit considered new fans.

When Gage had sat down again, Kashena and Sebastian came over to tell her they were leaving.

"When are you hitting Natalia's class?" Kashena asked.

"Probably tomorrow after work," Gage said.

"You better redeem us butches, that's all I'm tellin' ya," Kashena said.

Gage laughed. "I'll work on that."

"Be prepared—Nat's really beaten a number of asses in her day," Sebastian said. "She's had more people pass out in her class than any other class I've ever seen."

"That's comforting," Gage said, looking unafraid.

"What class is this?" Kit couldn't help but ask.

"It a cardio dance class that one of Kash and Baz's friends teaches," Gage explained.

"And you're going to do the class?" Kit asked, her tone indicating that she didn't understand why this was a big deal.

"It's not that simple," Kashena said, grinning. "Ya see, Natalia's cardio dance class is killer, and not only did your boss bet Natalia she could do the class, she also bet her that she would do it without missing too many steps. No one can do that." Kashena shook her head at Gage. "She's gonna kill you."

"Thanks for the confidence," Gage said.

"Anytime," Kashena said. "Either way the drinks are free Friday night."

"Why's that?" Kit asked.

"'Cause if Gage loses she buys drinks for the group, and if Nat loses she buys."

"Oh, that's handy," Kit said, laughing. "Now I'm wishing I was part of your group."

"Sebastian's an honorary lesbian. We could make you one too," Kashena said, winking.

Kit laughed.

Kashena and Sebastian left shortly after that.

"I think I might have to come watch this," Kit said to Gage.

"That would mean you'd have to let me give you a ride home tomorrow night too," Gage said, grinning.

"True," Kit said. "I think it might be worth it."

Later, Kit saw how personable Gage really was—she talked to everyone, from the lowest clerical to the highest executive. She traded jokes and stories and seemed to know everyone's name, division and rank in the department. It was something Kit had to ask about the second they were back in her vehicle.

"Okay, so how did you do that?" Kit asked as they stood at the back of the truck.

"Do what?" Gage pulled off her paint-stained BDU shirt, folded it stain side in, and put it in her bag.

When Kit didn't answer her, Gage turned to the girl. Kit's mouth was agape, her eyes on the tattoos on Gage's shoulders.

"They're tattoos…" Gage said.

"I know, but… wow," Kit said, her voice awed. "That's some serious work."

"It took a while," Gage said.

"I'll bet. Celtic crosses?"

"I'm Irish."

"Makes sense," Kit said. "They're really detailed."

"And hiding some nasty scars on the right shoulder," Gage said mildly.

Kit looked closer. "Can't really see them," she said, shaking her head.

"And that's the idea," Gage replied, opening the passenger door for Kit. "It saves me from having to explain too much. Now, what were you asking before the tattoos distracted you? How did I do what?"

"How did you know everyone's names, and things like that Ruth's son is in the infantry?"

Gage grinned as she walked around and climbed into the truck on the driver's side.

"I'll tell you a little secret," Gage said. "I have a photographic memory. I remember everything I see."

Kit stared at Gage, trying to decide if she was kidding or not, but decided that she didn't look like she was.

"So that 'walk' you took the other day…"

"Was to learn names, faces and things about the people who work for me."

"People thought you were spying on them," Kit said derisively.

Gage shrugged. "In a way I was."

"But not to see if they were working or not," Kit pointed out.

"True, but I did note the ones who didn't seem to be working," Gage said.

"Were those the ones you invited to succeed elsewhere?"

"Yep."

"So Shenin, Kashena and Harley…" Kit began, glancing over at Gage.

"All *family*," Gage said.

Kit nodded, understanding what Gage meant.

"Any problem with that?" Gage asked.

"Why would there be a problem?" Kit asked. "I used to be *family*."

Gage's head snapped around to her. "Excuse me?"

"Yeah, I was all *family* all the time, before Jack."

"So he was the first man you slept with?"

Kit nodded.

"Was he that good?" Gage asked, her expression showing that she had a hard time believing that of any man.

"Unfortunately, no," Kit said, wrinkling up her nose, "but my daughter was conceived on that very first try, so…"

Gage winced. "I'm hoping he got better with time?" she asked hopefully.

Kit pulled a face, shaking her head.

"Ouch," Gage said. "So why do you stay?"

Kit looked hesitant, then shrugged. "It's so hard financially to raise a child these days. Day care alone is more than my rent."

Gage gave her a searching look. "Can I ask you something?"

"Sure."

"And I want you to be completely honest with me," Gage said seriously.

"Okay…" Kit said, even more hesitant now.

"He gets violent with you, doesn't he?"

Kit's eyes widened, her nostrils flaring in shock. "How…"

"I saw bruises on your arms one day in the office," Gage said. "I also recognize the signs. Like meeting me downstairs this morning." Gage looked over at Kit again. "Is he giving you shit about the lesbian you work for?"

Kit pressed her lips together. Gage had just hit the nail on the head. Jack had been hammering at her about that "lesbo" she was working for and saying that Gage was hot, and on and on. She'd been afraid to have Gage come to the door for fear of what kind of stupid thing Jack would say to her boss.

She nodded rather than answering. She was completely mortified that Gage knew about the abuse.

Gage reached over and touched Kit's hand, her face serious as they sat at a red light.

"I don't have to tell you what a dangerous situation that is, Kit," she said, her voice soft. "For you and for Caitlyn."

Kit nodded again, doing her best to hold back tears of shame.

"Aw, damn it, Kit, I'm sorry," Gage said, seeing Kit's face.

She pulled the Escalade over to the side of the road and got out, walking around to the passenger's side and opening the door. She stepped up onto the running board and took Kit in her arms, hugging her.

"I didn't mean to upset you," Gage said softly. "I just saw too many women hurt or killed at the hands of abusive men in my career, and I don't want that to happen to you."

Kit nodded against her shoulder.

Gage pulled back. "I need you to promise me something."

"What?" Kit asked, brushing at the tears on her cheeks.

"I want you to promise me that you'll seriously think about changing that situation," Gage said, then grinned. "Hell, come back to our side." She winked. "We have cookies."

Kit laughed at that, then gave Gage a hesitant look. "I don't want you to think badly of me…"

"No," Gage said. "I don't, okay? I just don't want you hurt."

Kit bit her lip, nodding.

Gage took the younger girl's hand in hers. "If anything, and I mean anything, happens and you need something, I expect you to call me, no matter what time it is and no matter what you need. Do you understand me?"

Kit nodded, blinking a couple of times.

"If he puts his hands on you again, I better get a call," Gage clarified.

Kit's eyes widened.

"If I see bruises on you again, he and I are going to have a conversation, and he's not going to like the way it's going to end for him, okay?" Gage said.

"I wouldn't want to involve you in that. It's not your responsibility."

Gage canted her head at Kit. "Did you hang around many butches while you were gay?"

Kit chuckled at the phrase "while you were gay." "Some."

"Then you should know that we take the protection of people we care about very seriously."

Kit shook her head. "The butches I hung around weren't really like that."

Gage gave her a deadpan look. "Baby butches?" she asked disparagingly.

"They were young, yes. I was only nineteen."

"Okay, well, you definitely need to come to the bar with me Friday night. You need to meet some real butches, and then you'll probably understand." Gage grinned.

Kit bit her lip. "It would be really fun to be around *family* again…" she said wistfully.

"So come," Gage said. "I'll even pay for the babysitter."

Kit laughed. "My mom loves babysitting, so there's no need."

"Then come."

"Okay," Kit said. "But you need to win that bet tomorrow."

"Oh, I will."

***

The next night, everyone watched in awe as Gage nailed almost every step of Natalia's routines. Jericho leaned on the half wall next to the dance floor, her eyes narrowed.

"I think I see what's going on here," Jericho said.

"What?" Quinn asked.

Jericho looked over at Kit. "She has a photographic memory, doesn't she?"

Kit pressed her lips together, her blue eyes dancing.

"Son of a…" Jericho breathed. "Nat's in deep shit."

"So what does that mean?" Quinn asked. "How's that helping her with the steps?"

"Watch," Jericho said as the rest of the bois moved to listen in. "See how she misses the first step, but she never takes her eyes off Nat. Once she knows the step, she can do it every time. She sees the move and she can do it. I mean, I gotta give it to her—she's able to *do* the moves, that's not easy either, but she's memorizing the routines at an impossibly fast pace, because once she sees it she's got it," Jericho said, her grin wide.

"Genius," Kai said.

"Fecking brilliant!" Quinn said so loudly that Natalia came over and shushed her.

"How does losing feel, chica?" Quinn asked, her green eyes sparkling.

Natalia smacked Quinn's arm. "Something like that." She went back to the class.

"Evil little sprite," Quinn muttered, even as she smiled.

"You should know that by now," Remington said.

"Irishwomen learn slow," Jet said.

"That one doesn't," Kit said proudly.

The bois in the group exchanged looks. They liked the cute little soft butch Gage had brought with her. Kashena had informed them all that Kit was Gage's assistant and married to a MAN, but it didn't keep them all from thinking the girl was cute.

"Your boss is kicking ass," Kashena said from Kit's right.

"Isn't she?" Kit said, grinning.

"Looks like Nat's buying tomorrow night," Sebastian said, coming up behind Kashena and Kit.

On the way home from the class, Gage's phone rang.

"Sorry, excuse me." Gage hit the hands-free on her steering wheel to answer the phone. "Hey, babe, what's up?" she asked, having seen that it was Mark.

"Hey, Mom," Mark said, sounding upset.

"What's going on, babe?" Gage asked, worried immediately.

"Now she's saying she's having the baby but then she's moving away." He sounded like he was near tears.

"Oh, babe… That's not going to happen, okay?"

"What if it does, Mom? She's going to take my baby away from me."

"No, Mark, she's not," Gage said seriously. "You have rights as the father of that child, and she's not going anywhere with your baby, do you understand?"

"But, Mom—"

"I will take her ass to court so fast it'll make her head spin, Mark. She's not going anywhere with my grandchild and your baby. That's that."

"Okay," Mark said, his voice small.

Kit glanced over at Gage and saw her grimace.

"Where are you, babe?" Gage asked.

"In the car," he replied.

"Do you want to come stay at the house tonight?" Gage asked. "I could use the company—you know how big Grandma's house is…" She let her voice trail off as she silently hoped he'd accept her offer.

"Yeah, Mom, I think I will. Thanks."

"You still have your key? I'm not home just yet."

"Yeah," Mark said.

"Did you eat yet?"

"No," came the simple reply.

"Okay. When you get to the house, there's like a thousand takeout menus in the kitchen drawer on the island. They all have my credit card on file, so order whatever you want, and get me whatever. You know what I eat."

"Anything?" Mark asked, his grin evident in his voice.

"I swear to God, Marcus Nikitas Menasis, if you get Indian food and smell up Grandma's house with curry, you're explaining it to her!"

Mark started laughing. Gage just shook her head, smiling, but glad that Mark sounded like he was in a better mood now.

"I'll see you soon, babe. Drive carefully, okay?"

"Will do, Mom. Love you," Mark said.

"Love you too."

After they hung up, Kit glanced over at Gage. Gage caught the querying look.

"Ask," Gage told her.

"Ask what?"

"The question you wanted to ask that first night."

Kit's eyes widened, then she nodded.

"Okay. Mark… how?" Kit asked.

Gage smiled. "I was actually married to a man for about twelve years," she said, knowing she was going to shock the girl and holding up her hand to forestall Kit's outburst. "Not for the same reason you were," she told her. "I got married on purpose, to hide my sexuality."

"Okay…" Kit said. "Did your husband know?"

"Oh, yeah. Nick was gay and in the military too, so… it worked," Gage said, shrugging. "But the one thing he did want was a child. So we did the insemination thing, with his sperm, my egg, and I had Mark."

"Wow," Kit said, her eyes still wide.

Gage grinned, knowing it wasn't what Kit had expected at all. Most people wouldn't have guessed it.

"How did that work with both of you in the military? Was he never deployed?"

"Nick and I had a house in Greece. We kept Mark there and traded off on deployments so one of us was with him all the time."

"But eventually you got divorced…" Kit said.

"No," Gage said. "Nick was killed in Afghanistan when Mark was ten."

"Oh my God."

"Yeah," Gage said. "That's when I left the military and moved back to the States with Mark."

"Alone?" Kit asked, thinking of her comment the day before about how hard it was to raise a child on her own.

"Actually, no," Gage said. "My gunner, co-pilot and best friend, Jocelyn, quit the military with me and got me to move to San Francisco. She helped me raise Mark."

"Now that's a best friend," Kit said, amazed.

Gage chuckled. "Yeah, she said she couldn't co-pilot for anyone else, so she had to quit. I just think she didn't think I could handle Mark alone."

"I doubt that. You seem pretty good at the mothering thing," Kit said.

"Oh, I wouldn't have been then," Gage said. "I don't cook, I don't eat healthy, and I wouldn't have known how to do laundry if my life had depended on it."

"You never did laundry?"

"I left high school and my mom's house of maids and butlers, went to West Point, and then was in the Army, so I never had to do my own laundry really."

"You went to West Point?" Kit blinked a couple of times, shocked that Gage would mention such a prestigious college in passing like that.

"Caught that, huh? Should have stuck with 'college.'"

"That's really amazing," Kit said, shaking her head.

"It's a military college. It's not that big of a deal."

"Right, sure, okay," Kit said.

There didn't seem to be an end to the ways that Gage McGinnis was astonishing. There was so much more to the OES director than anyone knew. She felt fairly privileged that she was getting to learn so much. That night when Gage dropped her off, Kit found herself feeling a bit sad, wishing for a different life.

She went into her apartment, hugging her daughter and thanking the babysitter who was with her. She was told that Jack was "out." Kit made a point of putting Caitlyn to bed early and going to bed early herself, wanting to be asleep when Jack got home from the bar. It didn't matter; she woke to the feeling of his hard-on pressing against her.

She gritted her teeth the entire time he had sex with her, her eyes closed, just wanting it to be over quickly. She knew better than to fight him or try to put him off—that was when he got nasty and violent sometimes, especially when he was drunk. She knew he was drunk because it took him forever to get done. After he passed out, she got out of bed and took a shower, wanting his smell off of her. It seemed worse every time—she realized that it was because she was now comparing him to what she imagined someone like Gage or Kashena would be like…

The next morning she found that she was sore, and she moved more gingerly than she normally would. Gage noted it the minute she walked into the office.

"Kit?" Gage called from her office.

Kit got up and walked to Gage's office door, her notepad in hand, doing her best to appear normal.

"Yes?" she said from the doorway.

Gage gave her a pointed look. "Come in and shut the door, please."

Kit bit her lip and did as Gage told her to, then walked over and sat in the chair in front of Gage's desk, unable to stop the wince caused by the pain from sitting. Gage was up and out of her chair and walking around the desk immediately. She leaned against it, her hands on either side of her.

"What happened?" Gage asked, her green eyes searching Kit.

"Nothing," Kit said. "I'm fine, really."

"Kit…" Gage cautioned.

"Honestly," Kit said. "It was just… sex." Her voice was quiet on the last word.

Gage's expression was pained. "But…"

"Consensual," Kit said placatingly.

"Because you don't want to cause a fight."

Kit looked at Gage and blew her breath out. "Basically."

"Jesus, Kit," Gage breathed. "That's no life."

"But it's my life," Kit said.

Gage grimaced again but nodded, obviously accepting what she was saying.

"Okay, so we leave tomorrow, right?" Gage said.

"Yeah," Kit said.

"And you're gonna come out with me tonight, right?"

Kit smiled. "Yes," she said. "I already asked my mom to pick up Caitlyn from school. I brought my clothes with me to change into, and maybe you could just swing back by and get me or…" Kit realized she hadn't thought about the fact that they usually left the office around six and most clubs didn't get going till around nine.

"Or," Gage said, "we can run by my house, and we can both change there, and then I can treat you to dinner, and then we go to the Club."

"So like a real night out? Like real adults?" Kit asked, smiling widely.

Gage chuckled. "Just like real adults."

After work that evening, Gage drove them to her mother's house. As she got off the Hollywood freeway to go up into the west hills, she glanced over at Kit.

"Something I should probably tell you, so you don't have a heart attack. My mother's house is kind of… well, big."

"What does that mean?" Kit sensed that Gage was trying to tell her something more than that the house was "big."

Gage sighed. "Have you ever heard of Lenna McGinnis?"

Kit looked like she was thinking about it, but then nodded slowly. "She's a singer, right? One of the older-time rocker girls, kinda like

Melissa Etheridge…" Her eyes widened as she made the connection. "Your mom is a rock star?"

Gage laughed. "Yeah, and the house I'm staying in is hers—well, the one she owns here in LA. She's in London at this point."

"So when you say her house is big, you mean really big," Kit said.

"Thirteen thousand square feet, eight bedrooms, nine bathrooms," Gage said, grinning.

"There's more bathrooms than there are bedrooms?"

"Pool house," Gage added.

"Oh, my," Kit said. "That's not something that's in the press release, huh?"

"I try to keep my mom's identity on the low key," Gage said. "Saves me a lot of trouble."

"Kind of like the tattoos? You don't want people asking too many questions."

"Exactly."

"Wouldn't want too many people calling you a hero, or the daughter of a rock star…" Kit said, grinning.

Gage gave her a vile look. "Don't make me fire you."

"It's pretty hard to fire a state employee," Kit told her.

"Try me," Gage said, grinning.

Kit widened her eyes. "Okay, I take it back."

At the house, Kit couldn't help but be impressed. The house was Arts and Crafts style, built in the early 1900s. The redwood staircase with recessed coffered ceilings with incredible stained glass insets was just the beginning of the amazingly beautiful home. Gage showed Kit around, watching as she grew more and more dazzled. There was a salon with a marble fireplace surrounded by finely carved wood and a ceiling painted with intricate gold-leaf patterns. Every piece of furniture looked incredibly expensive. Then there were the views from every huge picture window, the city down to the ocean, amazing, beautiful views.

"This is the most astounding house I've ever been in in my entire life," Kit breathed as Gage showed her the master bedroom.

It was bigger than her apartment, with an adjacent sitting room-slash-office. There was a wall of windows, beautifully framed with carved wood. There was a huge sleigh bed and expensive-looking furniture throughout the room. The bathroom and dressing room were huge as well.

"Isn't it kind of weird being in this huge house by yourself?" Kit asked.

"Yes!" Gage said, laughing. "It's why I tried to tell my mother no when she insisted I stay here, but she hates the idea of me renting a place. And she's kind of a steamroller when it comes to her only daughter, so… she wins every time."

"Are you an only child?"

"Yep," Gage said. "You?"

"No," Kit said. "I have two brothers, both older."

"And your mom, obviously," Gage said, sitting on the bed.

"Yeah," Kit said. "My dad's been out of the picture for years now."

"Yeah, my dad hasn't been around for years either. I see him occasionally, but my mom can't stand him, so she doesn't let him around here."

"Oh," Kit said, grimacing.

"Well, let's get changed and figure out where you want to grab dinner," Gage said. "As you saw, pretty much every room has a bathroom, so just pick one," she said with a smile.

Kit picked the bedroom that was just down the hall from the master. Standing in the bathroom, she looked at the granite countertops, the cream-colored vanity with the carved handles, and the wood-framed mirrors and beautiful brushed-copper fixtures. She couldn't imagine being around such beautiful things all the time. She quickly changed her clothes and touched up her makeup, darkening her eyeliner a bit and using a darker lip color as well. She was dressed in black slim-fit jeans with the hem rolled up to the top of her black-and-white high-top sneakers accented with silver and rhinestones. She wore a white button-up shirt whose collar was also tipped with silver and rhinestones, and a black jean jacket.

Gage looked like the consummate butch in snug-fitting faded jeans, black combat boots, a black tank top with a rainbow bar across the front, and a black-and-blue flannel shirt over the top. She wore her usual black watch and a couple of black chains, one with her black dog tags, the other with a set of interconnected rainbow rings dangling from it. Her hair, completely loose for once, was the only thing on the woman that looked feminine.

When Gage saw Kit, she smiled. "Cute."

"Cute?" Kit asked.

"Yeah, in a soft-butch kind of way."

"Some of us can't pull off full-on butch," Kit said, gesturing to Gage.

"I've been at it longer, baby girl," Gage said, winking at her.

Kit laughed.

"Wait till you see Jos. Now she's got butch down," Gage said.

"I'm going to meet her?" Kit asked.

"Yeah, she lives in San Francisco still," Gage said. "She's going to come hang out at the hotel with us."

"Cool," Kit said, smiling. She was very interested in meeting Gage's best friend; she'd heard enough about her to want to know what she was like.

"Okay, so dinner," Gage said, pulling out her phone. "What do you like? Italian? French? American? Asian? Steak? Salad? What?"

"Um," Kit stammered. "I've never had French food…"

"Oh lord. Yeah, you really need to meet Jos. She's the foodie," Gage said as she tapped information into her phone. "Okay, I know a place… and I just got us a reservation. Let's go."

They drove for a half hour. Once at the restaurant, Gage gave the keys to the valet with a wink. "Tip in it for ya if I don't have any scratches," she told the blond girl.

"You got it," the girl said, smiling warmly, her eyes staring right back into Gage's.

As they walked into the restaurant, Kit glanced at Gage. "You did catch that flirt, right?"

Gage smirked. "I'm not blind."

"You just didn't really react, so I wasn't sure," Kit said, her tone teasing.

"I'll wait to see what condition my truck comes back in before I react," Gage said with a lopsided smile.

Kit looked around as they walked to an elevator. "Where is this place?"

"On the roof." Gage smiled as she hit the button for the top floor.

"Wow," Kit said, thinking the view would likely be amazing.

She was not wrong. The restaurant was called Perch, because it perched at the top of an old office building in downtown Los Angeles. The views from the top were incredible.

"It's not too cold tonight. Do you want to sit outside?" Gage asked.

"Yes, please," Kit said, smiling as she gazed around her.

When they were seated, Kit continued to stare, her eyes wide with wonder. "This place is beautiful, Gage."

Gage grinned, liking that Kit was so wide eyed and innocent. Other women she'd been with or around wouldn't have looked twice at the scenery. It was nice to see someone so unused to beautiful things seeing them for the first time. That had been the case at the house as well. Kit seemed to take in literally everything she saw, as if she was storing it up to think about later. It was very endearing.

The waitress came over to the table, smiling at them both. "Can I get you something to drink?"

"I'll have a beer," Gage said. "Whatever's on tap."

"We have a nice winter ale," the waitress offered helpfully.

"Sure."

"And for you?" the waitress asked Kit.

"Just water for me, thank you."

The waitress nodded, then walked away.

"You are allowed to drink, you know," Gage told Kit.

"I just didn't…" Kit said. "I'm not sure what to drink. I really haven't ever had alcohol."

"Seriously?"

"I was twenty when I got married, so I've never really gone out when I was old enough to drink."

"Oh, honey, we're going to have to fix that," Gage said. "Do you like sweet stuff? Fruity stuff? Or are you more of a savory, smokey, non-sweet kind of drinker, do you think?"

"I don't have any idea," Kit said.

When the waitress returned with Gage's beer, Gage handed it to Kit. "Try it."

Kit tasted the ale and made a face.

"That's a definite no." Chuckling, Gage looked at the waitress. "Okay, we need to try a few things. Can you bring her a shot of Baileys, a shot of Jack, and a margarita?"

"Sure," the waitress said. "Did you want to order food? Or are we just doing alcohol tonight?"

Gage laughed. "No, we're going to eat too. Give us a minute with the menu."

"You got it," the waitress said.

A few minutes later, she came back with the drinks for Kit.

"Okay, so just sip," Gage told Kit. "Start with the Jack Daniels," she said, handing the girl the shot.

Kit sipped it and again made a face.

"Okay, no Jack." Gage took the shot from her and tossed it back.

"I guess you drink Jack Daniels?" Kit asked as she sipped the Baileys.

"Sweetheart, I was in the Army. I drink anything," Gage said, laughing.

"I like this," Kit said, indicating the Baileys.

"Okay, what about the margarita?"

Kit sipped the margarita. "This is pretty good too."

"Okay, so the girly fruity drinks," Gage said with a straight face, making Kit give her a dirty look.

"Hey…" Kit said, laughing. Gage just chuckled.

In the end they shared a few different entrées, and Kit found that Gage was a lot of fun outside of the office too.

Later at the Club, Gage was greeted by the group, and she introduced Kit to everyone that hadn't already met her. Gage informed the group that this was Kit's first night of drinking. That had shots being brought to the table constantly. Everyone took pity on Natalia, and by extension Raine, who made the steady money in their household, and bought shots for Kit on the side.

Memphis, who had apparently adored Kit on sight, dragged her out onto the dance floor and kept her there for her entire break.

"I believe I may have lost my wife," Kieran said, grinning as she watched Memphis with Kit.

"Nah, they're too much alike," Gage said. "They may become buddies though."

"I'd be okay with that," Kieran said, smiling.

Memphis was very attached to Remington, Quinn and Kai, but she had few people as young as she was to hang out with, other than Kieran. Kieran was wise enough to know that Memphis needed more friends their age. Kit was young enough to fit that bill.

"So you're married to a guy?" Memphis asked. They were out on the patio, and Memphis was smoking.

"Yeah," Kit said. "Crazy, I know, but when I got pregnant, I freaked out. When he asked me to marry him, I thought it was the right thing to do."

"And what do you think now?" Memphis asked.

"I think I miss this life," Kit said, smiling wistfully. "I can't even say I miss it as much as I never got to this part, you know?"

"The fun drinking-partying-dancing part?" Memphis asked.

"Exactly!" Kit said, laughing. "I also miss the hope of what they all have," Kit said, looking inside toward the group. "And what you and Kieran have… you know?"

Memphis nodded. "Yeah, I get that too," she said. "Kier was with me for the worst time in my life, and I don't know that I would have made it through it without her. Now I know I have someone that I can always come home to, you know? And that's awesome."

"Yeah, I bet," she said. "With Jack I never know what I'm coming home to. Nice guy, mean guy, guy that calls my boss a dyke and says I just want to fuck her."

"He says that he thinks you just want to do Gage?"

"Yeah," Kit said, "that it's got to be the only reason I want to work for her."

"Is it?" Memphis asked. "She's pretty hot."

Kit laughed. "Yeah, she is pretty hot, that's true," she said honestly. "But she's got an amazing way of doing her job. You had to see her earlier this week. The way she talks to people, to employees... She makes people feel like they want to work harder for her, because they want to help her do what she's doing. That's a really amazing thing. I was so proud to work for her that day." She shook her head. "She's committed to what we're doing in that agency, and it feels really great to work there right now, and that's because of her. She's an incredible leader."

Memphis nodded, looking impressed by what Kit had said. "Well, I liked her almost as fast as I liked you, and everyone tells me that I'm a good judge of character."

"Well, you are when it comes to her. And me too, of course," Kit said with a laugh.

"That's an interesting dynamic," Remington said to Jericho, looking out onto the patio where Memphis and Kit sat.

"Might be good for both of them," Jericho said, having heard from Gage a little about Kit.

Remington glanced over at Gage, who was also looking toward the patio.

"Think anything's happening there?' Remington asked, nodding toward Gage.

"Don't know," Jericho said. "But at this point I think Gage just wants to give the girl the life back, you know?"

"She's actually married to a man, but a lesbian?" Remington had heard the scuttlebutt about Kit.

"Yeah, and it doesn't sound like a good situation," Jericho said.

"Good thing she's part of our group then, huh?" Remington said, grinning.

Becoming a member of the group meant gaining the influence, assistance and the backup of the group. The members were fiercely loyal and would show up for any one of them anytime, anywhere. They'd gone to the mat for each other quite often. With so many of them in law enforcement or the entertainment industry, it was very definitely a good thing to become a part of the group. Kit Landry had no idea how many friends and backers she'd just acquired.

Chapter 4

Gage and Kit got to San Francisco at 3 p.m. the next day. It was a Saturday, but Gage had wanted to get there early so they'd have time to settle in before the conference officially started on Monday morning. She also wanted to be there for the cocktail hour on Sunday night, to get a chance to figure out the "lay of the land," as she called it.

They were at the Fairmont Heritage right off of Ghirardelli square. Gage had asked Kit to book them there as they had suites; it would make communication between them easier during the conference. It became more needed when mudslides were reported in the Sierras just east of Sacramento shortly after they arrived.

The room had two separate bedrooms, a kitchen, dining room and living room. There were views of the San Francisco Bay from the living room. It was a very nice room. The price tag had been fairly steep too.

Because they'd stayed out late the night before, and Gage had already been having issues with sleeping during the week, she turned in early that first night. Kit was watching TV when there was a knock on the door. Opening it, she stood staring openmouthed at a tall dark-haired woman wearing faded jeans, brown cowboy boots, a burgundy tank top, and a jean jacket.

"Hi, I'm Gun," the woman said, smiling. "You must be Kit."

Kit smiled as she opened the door wider and motioned for her to come in.

"She always calls you Jos," Kit said.

"She's the only one that does," Jocelyn said, shaking her head.

"Well, she calls you Gun sometimes too, but I thought that was because you were her gunner."

"Well, my middle name is Gunnar too," Jocelyn said. "But I doubt she ever thinks about that."

Kit smiled. "She talks about you a lot."

"Where is Jock anyway?"

"Okay, explain that one," Kit said.

"What, Jock?" Jocelyn asked.

"Yeah."

"You know, like a jockey. The rider, the driver…"

"Oh." Kit nodded toward one of the bedrooms. "She's in there, maybe asleep, but she said to send you in when you got here."

"Uh-huh. I doubt she's asleep. She doesn't do that too well." Jocelyn grinned. "Your boss is kind of a control freak."

"Is she? I hadn't noticed," Kit said, grinning too.

Jocelyn laughed as she walked over to the bedroom door. "See you later," she said, then went inside.

Inside the room, Jocelyn looked over at the bed. Gage lay on her back, her left arm up over her head on the pillow, staring up at the ceiling. She was wearing a tank top and black pants, her trim figure and great curves on display nicely. There was no denying her best friend was one seriously hot woman. Walking over, Jocelyn leaned down and kissed Gage's right shoulder, where the scars from the accident were. Gage's eyes were already staring up at her.

"Hey…" she said, smiling at Jocelyn.

"How ya doin'?" Jocelyn said, scooting Gage over on the bed and sitting against the headboard, looking down at Gage.

Gage sat up. She looked far too sexy in her tousled state.

"Okay," Gage said, shrugging.

Jocelyn sensed immediately that all was not well.

"What's up, Jock?" she asked.

Gage shook her head, her eyes downcast. "I really think I might have fucked up this time."

"Not possible," Jocelyn said, leaning to the side to get under Gage's line of sight. "Tell me what's going on."

Gage leaned against Jocelyn, her head on Jocelyn's shoulder. It was her way of avoiding the topic and Jocelyn knew it. They'd been friends long enough to know that when something was bugging Gage, she had to drag it out of her, otherwise it would fester and eventually come out some other way. Gage McGinnis wasn't someone a person wanted to be around when she finally lost her cool. Jocelyn had seen it enough to want to avoid it if at all possible.

"Come on, Jock, talk to me." Jocelyn wrapped her arm around Gage's shoulders, pulling her in close.

"I have no fucking idea what I'm doing. I'm down five executives, I don't even have a co-pilot at this point…"

"How hard can that be?" Jocelyn said. "Finding some suits to fill some shoes."

Gage lifted her head. "You are kidding, right? These aren't just regular executive jobs, Gun. I need people who know their shit."

"And you got no options?" Jocelyn asked disbelievingly.

"Well, I do," Gage said, "for four out of the five, but the one I really need to fill is the chief deputy director."

"And there aren't any options?" Jocelyn repeated.

Gage looked pensive, her lips curling in dissatisfaction. "Just one."

"So then go with that one," Jocelyn said, holding up her hands in a gesture of futility.

Gage gave Jocelyn an amused look. "I would, but you'll probably say no."

Jocelyn stared back at her for a long moment, having to take a pause to absorb what Gage had just said. Then she shook her head.

"You're fuckin' crazy," she said.

"Maybe," Gage said, "but you're the only person I know that I trust to back me up."

"You can't call your pal Midnight and get some ideas from her?"

"I did, and she's where I got the idea for the other four, I'm poaching them from DOJ, but I can't just have anyone as my co-pilot, Gun… and you're the only one that I can think of for the job."

"I fucking hate LA," Jocelyn said.

Gage chuckled. "I know."

"How could you do that anyway? I don't work for the state."

"The same way Midnight appointed me, I can appoint you."

"I don't want to be a suit," Jocelyn said.

"You think I wear a suit? Ever?" Gage asked, giving her best friend a serious look.

Jocelyn narrowed her eyes. "You know what I mean, Jock."

"We make it what we want, Gun. The place is ours."

"But you answer to someone," Jocelyn said.

"We all do," Gage said. "But I can tell you, I'd rather answer to Midnight Chevalier over any man in politics any day of the week."

Gage gazed at Jocelyn for a moment, seeing the hesitation in her best friend's eyes and suddenly feeling bad for putting her on the spot. She let out a breath, dropping her head.

"Shit, I'm sorry, Jos," she said, sounding dejected. "You have a life here, and I'm trying to drag you around with me like I always do… You know, you're right, I can do this. I'm sorry. Forget I even asked you to do this. I'm good. I'll be fine."

Jocelyn looked over at Gage. She knew her best friend well enough to know she was now falling on her sword and being anything but honest.

"Don't do that," Jocelyn said.

"Do what?" Gage said, her eyes flicking from Jocelyn's to a spot just over her shoulder, which was a sure sign.

"You can't even look me in the eye, Jock. You're doing that shit you tried to do when Nick died, the 'I'll be fine on my own' shit."

"I would have been fine."

"Right, but I wouldn't have been," Jocelyn said. "Just like you're not now. You think I can't see the tension in you? You're like a guitar string that's been tightened about two too many turns and you're about to snap. You're not sleeping either, I can see that."

Gage had never liked how easy it was for Jocelyn to read her. She shifted her position on the bed slightly, her shoulder twitching.

"And that's you fighting the desire to argue with me," Jocelyn said.

In one fluid motion, Jocelyn sat up and slid her hand behind Gage's head. She brought her mouth down on Gage's, her lips demanding. Jocelyn felt Gage wanting to pull away, so she slid her other hand around the smaller woman's waist and pulled her closer. That did the trick—Gage moaned softly against her lips and then wrapped her arms around Jocelyn's neck.

Jocelyn slid her hand from Gage's waist and up Gage's torso, her thumb brushing up between them, rubbing over a hard nipple. Gage shuddered against her, her lips parting as Jocelyn's tongue slid between them to explore her mouth, while her hand moved down to pull at the bottom of the tank top Gage wore.

"No," Gage murmured. "Kit might need to update me…"

"Seriously?" Jocelyn moaned.

Gage nodded, her lips not leaving Jocelyn's.

Jocelyn slid her hand up under Gage's tank top, touching her and making her writhe. Gage straddled Jocelyn's hips, pressing closer. Jocelyn pulled the material of the tank top aside and moved her mouth over Gage's hard nipple. Gage groaned loudly, grasping Jocelyn's shoulder. Her body strained against Jocelyn's.

"Yeah, you'll be fine…" Jocelyn muttered.

"Shut up," Gage muttered back.

"So Kit's really cute…" Jocelyn said, her mouth at Gage's neck, close to her ear.

"Shut up, Gun," Gage growled, even though she moaned right after that as Jocelyn sucked at her skin.

"Come on, tell me you haven't thought about that," Jocelyn said, her voice low and husky.

"Shut up, Gun," Gage repeated, biting Jocelyn's neck and sliding herself against Jocelyn, making Jocelyn moan and shudder. "Looks like someone needs something too…"

"You really want to start with me?" Jocelyn raised an eyebrow at Gage. "You know I can hold out way longer than you can."

"Just fuck me and shut the hell up, okay?" Gage snapped.

Jocelyn chuckled as she slid her hand down inside the pants that Gage wore and touched her. Gage gasped.

"I fucking hate that you can do that," Gage groaned, moving her body against Jocelyn's fingers.

"You love that I can do that." Jocelyn moved her fingers exactly the way she knew Gage liked.

Gage was coming moments later, her mouth against Jocelyn's neck. After the waves of ecstasy calmed, Gage began kissing Jocelyn's neck, pressing herself against Jocelyn's body, moving seductively, using the body that she knew Jocelyn loved against her. Jocelyn's hands moved to her waist as she guided Gage's body against hers. Minutes later, Jocelyn gasped in her release, her hands grasping at Gage's waist.

"If you didn't have the damn sexiest body on the fucking planet, you totally wouldn't get away with that," Jocelyn said breathlessly, her head back against the headboard as she tried to catch her breath.

Gage chuckled, her head against Jocelyn's shoulder. "Uh-huh," she said, sounding unconvinced. "We both just know each other's triggers."

"That we do." Jocelyn slid her arms around Gage's shoulders as Gage settled comfortably against her. Gage straightened her legs and shifted slightly to Jocelyn's side. Jocelyn kicked off her boots, grinning.

"So what would I have to do as a chief deputy director of OES?" Jocelyn asked.

Gage shifted to look up at her. "Basically be my backup and help me run the place."

"That's all, huh?" Jocelyn said wryly.

Gage nodded. "But you'd only have to answer to me."

Jocelyn's lips twitched. Right now she was a sergeant with San Francisco PD. She'd never wanted to go any higher, not like Gage had. The fact was, her lieutenant was a complete asshole, and she wanted to shoot him regularly. Gage being her "boss" was very tempting. She didn't by any stretch of the imagination assume that Gage wouldn't call her to task if she did something wrong or stupid, but she and Gage knew how to work together to solve things. God knew how many times they'd done just that over the years of raising Mark with completely different views on parenting.

"I will think about it," Jocelyn told Gage, putting her finger to Gage's lips. "*Think* about it."

Gage kissed Jocelyn's finger. "Okay."

Gage put her head back down against Jocelyn's stomach, her arm thrown over Jocelyn's waist. She closed her eyes, breathing in the scent of her best friend. It was such a familiar scent that she couldn't even identify it anymore. Jocelyn had been her safety net for so many years now that it was easy to just curl up against her and drop off to sleep, which was what she did almost instantly.

Jocelyn lay in the semi-darkness of the room, gazing out at the Bay, her thoughts in turmoil. She did hate Los Angeles, but she also hated having Gage and Mark both down there when she was way up in San Francisco. Gage saying that she had a life was laughable—for Jocelyn, her life had moved to Los Angeles, first when Mark moved, then when Gage followed him to take this new job. Her life was now located in a city she abhorred, but the people she loved were more important than that to her. Gage had asked her for help, and no matter what, she'd always been there for her best friend. Gage was the one person in the world she would compromise everything for. It really sucked that they could never make it as a couple. Fate was a rather fickle bitch.

She was still awake, thinking about what all she'd need to do to make the transition to Los Angeles, when there was a light knock on the door.

"Yeah," she called as softly as she could.

Kit opened the door, her eyes taking in Jocelyn half reclining on the bed with Gage lying against her, her arm over Jocelyn possessively. She felt a stab of jealousy that she refused to acknowledge. It was easy to see how comfortable the two were together. Kit knew it was stupid to be jealous of that, but she was.

"I'm sorry," she whispered, grimacing because she felt like she was intruding.

"Don't worry about it." Jocelyn smiled. "Come on in." She looked down at Gage and touched her arm. "Jock?"

"Mmm?" Gage murmured tiredly.

"Director?" Kit said, reverting to formality in the face of the awkward situation she was in.

Gage rubbed her face, looking up at Kit. "What's up?"

Kit handed her the iPad on which she was getting updates about the mudslides. Gage took the iPad, moving to sit up against the headboard next to Jocelyn.

"What's this?" Jocelyn asked.

"There are mudslides happening in the Sierras," Gage said as she read over the latest report from the staff onsite.

"Okay, so what does OES handle in this kind of thing?" Jocelyn asked.

"Well, we handle things like notifications and working with the local departments to ensure they have the resources they need. In an emergency situation we have control over all state agencies, so if Cal Trans isn't responding quickly enough or with the resources they need, we can get ahold of other state agencies like Cal Fire and such if needed. Kit, I think I'm going to need to go up there in the morning. Can you arrange a helicopter?"

"Of course," Kit said. "Ride?"

"No, I'd rather fly myself if you can get me something; I have my private license on me if they need to see it."

"Okay," Kit said. "What kind of helicopter?"

"Doesn't matter. I can fly anything," Gage said.

Kit's eyes widened, and she looked at Jocelyn.

Jocelyn grinned. "Yeah, she really can. It's disgusting."

"If worse came to worse I could fly a fixed-wing, but they're a pain in the ass to land, and we'd still need to drive up, so…" Gage said.

"Helicopter it is," Kit said.

"Let's shoot for nine a.m.," Gage said. "And… what do you think, Jos? Oakland airport?"

"Probably be easier, less air traffic."

"Okay, so have them meet us at Oakland airport. Their helipad should work."

"Okay," Kit said.

"We'll need to leave here around eight to get over there." Gage glanced at Jocelyn, who nodded. "Got it?" she asked Kit with a grin.

"Yep," Kit said, smiling.

"And get some sleep somewhere in there too," Gage joked.

"Oh sure, you want everything," Kit said, rolling her eyes dramatically.

Gage laughed. "Thanks, Kit."

"Of course." Kit turned and left the room, closing the door softly behind her.

Jocelyn got up, taking off her jeans and unclipping her bra to pull it off from under her tank top then tossing it aside. Gage watched her.

"She sure is cute," Jocelyn said as she climbed back into bed.

"Shut up, Gun," Gage said as she lay back down.

Jocelyn chuckled as she lay down on her side, her hand resting on Gage's stomach. They fell asleep that way.

The next morning, Gage was up first, taking a shower and pulling on her jeans, her Army sweatshirt and her black combat boots. She pulled her hair up in a messy ponytail. When she walked out into the bedroom, Jocelyn was just stirring.

"You got about forty-five minutes," Gage told her.

"Yeah, yeah," Jocelyn said, turning over onto her back and stretching.

Gage smiled, recognizing the come-on, and shook her head.

"Not coming back over there," she said.

"Why not?" Jocelyn asked, grinning mischievously.

"You got forty-five minutes, Gun. Get it in gear." Gage walked out of the room.

She was still smiling when she walked into the kitchen area. Kit was already there making coffee.

"Good morning," Gage said to Kit.

"Morning."

"Did you sleep good?"

"I did," Kit said. "The bed is really comfortable. Did you sleep good?"

"Oh yeah," Gage said, nodding. "That's the sick thing—I always sleep better with Jos around. Habit, I guess, did it for so many years."

"You always slept together?" Kit asked.

"A lot, yeah."

"But you weren't a couple?"

"Nope," Gage said. "I know, it's crazy, but we just make way better friends than we do girlfriends."

Kit shook her head. She didn't understand it, and she couldn't imagine how they wouldn't make perfect girlfriends. She understood it less during the course of the day. She also saw her butch boss somewhat dominated by a stronger butch, which was odd as well.

Jocelyn drove them to Oakland airport; Gage sat in the passenger seat of the SUV she'd rented. The music that played on the SUV's stereo was Jocelyn's, and it was fairly different from Gage's music. They playfully argued about it on the way to the airport, and it was quite obvious they'd had the argument before.

"You're killin' me, Smalls," Gage said, her booted foot on the dashboard on the passenger's side.

"Driver picks the tunes. That's the rule, Jock, I can't help that," Jocelyn said.

"And you're picking the shit I hate, and you know it."

Jocelyn grinned. "No, I'm not picking what you hate. It's just what I have on here."

"I'm hatin' you right now, just know that," Gage said, smiling despite her words.

"How about this?" Jocelyn said, changing the song.

Bon Jovi's "Always Run to You" began.

"Oh yes, much better," Gage sighed, her head moving to the beat. "Brat."

"You say that like it's new."

"No, I know it's not new," Jocelyn said. "I just thought that being some high-up mucky-muck would make you less of a brat."

"Dream on, sweetie pie," Gage said, widening her eyes at Jocelyn as she grinned.

At the airport, Gage climbed into the helicopter Kit had acquired for them.

"Who'd we borrow an OH-58 from?" Gage asked Kit.

"Let's just say we owe Oakland PD a favor now," Kit said, grinning.

"Good deal," Gage said.

Kit sat in the back of the helicopter, putting on the headphones Gage handed her and listening to Gage and Jocelyn go over pre-flight.

"Okay, run her up," Gage said when they'd completed the checks.

"Coming up," Jocelyn said.

Minutes later they were in the air. Kit could hear the conversation with air traffic control, and it was quite evident that Gage and Jocelyn had been a team for a really long time—even if she hadn't known that already, she would have then.

When they reached the Sierra Nevada mountains, it wasn't long until they came upon the slide area.

"Jesus…" Jocelyn breathed, glancing over at Gage.

"Kit, have we gotten any new updates?" Gage asked. "Were any fatalities reported?"

Kit looked up the information and read it quickly. "No, there were a few dozen injuries, but no fatalities."

"Good, okay, thanks, Kit," Gage said, glancing over her shoulder.

Kit heard Jocelyn and Gage discussing where to land.

"I think I'll put her down right there," Gage was saying.

"You better watch those wires," Jocelyn said.

"You know me…"

Jocelyn shook her head as Gage lowered the helicopter to the ground, missing hanging wires by mere inches. "Like threading a fucking needle," Jocelyn muttered.

"Jealous?" Gage asked.

"As fuck," Jocelyn said. She turned her head toward Kit. "Your boss is a damned good pilot."

Kit smiled, inordinately proud of that fact.

The three of them got out of the helicopter, and a local news crew moved to film them. As they passed them, Jocelyn heard the reporter talking about the new director of OES piloting her own aircraft. Jocelyn rolled her eyes; these people reported on pretty much anything.

"You're making the news," Jocelyn told Gage as they made it down to the street.

"Not for the first time," Gage said, grinning.

They made their way over to a group of California Transportation workers who were huddled at the back of a truck, near a heater. It was cold in the Sierras. Snow hadn't fallen in a while; the warm winter storm that brought the rain that caused the mudslide had already passed, and a cold storm was headed in.

"Hey, guys, how's it going?" Gage asked as she walked up.

One man turned to her. "Miss, you need to get back behind the barriers," he snapped as he reached out his hand to seemingly escort her himself. "All of you need to get back."

Gage stopped, looking up at the guy. "I don't think you understand." She reached into her back pocket for her ID.

"Just get your pretty little ass back behind the barriers," the man said, his tone sharper and his movement more determined.

Jocelyn was in his face immediately. "You need to back up, and I mean now," she said in a low voice.

"Who the fuck do you think you are?" the man said, giving Jocelyn an upbraiding look.

"I think I'm the one that's going to put you down if you try to touch her again, and I *know* she's the director of OES and therefore temporarily your boss, so you might want to back the fuck up right now," Jocelyn said, backing the man up with every step she took.

The man looked from Jocelyn to Gage, who smiled icily.

He held his hands up. "I didn't know."

"Well, maybe before you try to manhandle a woman, you should find out who she is first," Jocelyn snapped.

"Easy, Gun," Gage said, putting her hand to Jocelyn's arm.

Jocelyn glanced at Gage, her lips twitching, and Gage could see she really wanted to continue to teach this guy a lesson. Gage shook her head slightly, her green eyes staring directly into Jocelyn's. Jocelyn finally blew her breath out and stepped back.

It was always a mistake for a man to try to grab at or in any way manhandle a woman in Jocelyn's presence. She would not tolerate anyone touching a woman roughly; it was one part of her very butch personality that was extremely strong. Gage had seen Jocelyn take down a number of men over the years for doing just that. She'd also seen Jocelyn take down a few other butch women for the same thing. Man or woman, you didn't mistreat a woman in Jocelyn's presence unless you wanted to deal with one very strong, very mean butch.

They checked out the slide area. Gage stopped and talked to people who'd lost homes.

"I'm sorry this happened," Gage told one family. "We'll make sure you get all the help you need to rebuild and live in the meantime."

The woman, holding a child, nodded. "Thank you, ma'am."

Another child, who had walked up to them as they talked to another family, tapped Gage on the leg. Gage glanced down at the boy, then kneeled to look him in the eye.

"Hi," Gage said, smiling at him.

"Are you the boss?" he asked, his brown eyes searching her face.

"To some people, yes," Gage said. "Did you need someone in charge?"

The boy nodded, looking worried.

"Okay, you can talk to me, and I'll see what I can help with."

"Did you come in that?" The boy pointed to the helicopter.

"Yeah," Gage said.

"Are you a pilot?"

"I am." Gage glanced up at Kit and Jocelyn, who were watching the conversation avidly.

"Can you use that to help me find my dog?" the boy asked.

"You lost your dog?" Gage asked with a meaningful look at Kit.

"Yeah. He's a German Shepherd, named Shep," the boy said.

Kit looked up the number to the local shelter and stepped away to call them.

"Well, I don't know how much good the helicopter would be to find him, because I can't fly too low around here," Gage said. "But that doesn't mean we can't help you find him."

"How long ago did you see Shep?" Jocelyn asked, kneeling as well.

"It was last night, when I went to bed," the boy said. "He was outside."

"Was he on a chain or anything?" Jocelyn asked.

"No, he was loose, but he never goes far…"

Gage stood up and walked over to Kit as Jocelyn asked the boy more questions.

"What's your name?" Jocelyn asked, knowing Gage wanted her to keep the boy occupied.

"Tommy. What's yours?"

"Gun," Jocelyn said.

"Really?" the boy asked, his eyes wide.

Jocelyn smiled, nodding. "You know why that's my name?"

"Why?" Tommy asked, looking excited now.

"Cause I was a gunner on a helicopter."

"Really?" Tommy asked. "What kind of helicopter?"

"An AH-64 Apache helicopter. Do you know what those look like?"

Tommy shook his head. "Uh-uh."

Jocelyn took out her phone and pulled up a photo of her and Gage in front of their chopper.

"That's so cool," Tommy said, touching the picture reverently. He pointed to the bottom of the helicopter. "What's that?"

"That's a Hellfire missile."

"Cool…" Tommy said, looking really impressed.

Jocelyn glanced up as Gage walked back over to them.

"I got good news," Gage said, smiling. "We found Shep. He's down at the shelter—they're holding on to him for you."

Tommy gazed up at Gage as if she was the new messiah. "You found him?"

"Well, my assistant Kit did," Gage said, nodding to Kit, who was walking up to them.

Tommy threw his arms around Kit, hugging her around the waist. Kit laughed softly as she wrapped her arms around the boy.

Gage leaned over to Jocelyn as she stood up. "See if one of our Cal Trans friends can break loose a truck to take him down to get his dog."

"You got it," Jocelyn said.

"Be nice."

"Yeah, yeah," Jocelyn said as she walked away.

Twenty minutes later, Tommy and his mother were on their way to the local shelter, but not before Tommy had hugged Kit again and also hugged both Jocelyn and Gage, thanking them profusely. His mother had also thanked them and later gave an interview to the local news to tell them about how the director of OES and her "staff" had taken the time to help her son locate his dog. She'd gone on to say how grateful she was to them, that the family dog was responsible for protecting them from her abusive ex-husband and that losing him would have been devastating to the family.

Two hours later, Gage and Jocelyn piloted them out of the area.

"Okay, I admit it," Jocelyn said to Gage over the mic. "That was pretty cool."

"I can't guarantee that level of cool every time," Gage said, grinning. "And Kit, you did an amazing job back there," she added, glancing over her shoulder at Kit.

"Thanks." Kit smiled, so happy to work for someone that gave her credit for things she did.

When they got back to Oakland, they picked up the rental vehicle, and Jocelyn drove them back into the city, suggesting they grab dinner before they went back to the hotel, since none of them had eaten since breakfast that morning.

"Morton's?" Gage asked hopefully.

"Always the carnivore," Jocelyn said.

Gage grinned. "I'm paying."

"Then you're on."

"Steak okay with you, Kit?" Gage asked.

"Sounds wonderful," Kit said.

Twenty minutes later, they drove up to Morton's Steakhouse and valeted the SUV. Walking inside, Kit felt completely underdressed. The place was very nice, and they were all wearing jeans. It didn't seem to matter to the staff, who greeted Jocelyn and Gage by name.

"Welcome back, ladies," the waiter said when he came up to the table, smiling at them both.

"Hey, Tim," Gage said. "Can I get my usual?"

"Of course." Tim looked at Jocelyn. "You want your usual too, Gun?"

"You bet."

"Kit, what do you want to drink?" Gage asked. "They have a really good Moscato wine here that you might like."

"Okay, I'll try that," Kit said.

As she scanned the menu, Kit noticed a couple of things—one, that neither Gage nor Jocelyn was looking at the menu, and two, that the steaks were outrageously expensive.

"Kit..." Gage warned as she saw Kit's eyes widen dramatically as they moved over the right side of the menu where the prices were located. "Just order whatever you want. Don't sweat the prices."

"I've never eaten a steak that expensive before," Kit said, shaking her head.

Jocelyn grinned. "Jock used to come here so often, she has her own wine locker."

"Seriously?" Kit asked, looking at Gage.

"I like a good steak," she said matter-of-factly.

"Holy cow," Kit said.

Jocelyn laughed. "Exactly!"

Kit smiled at the pun she'd unintentionally made.

A few minutes later, Tim came back. He handed Kit her glass of wine, handed Gage a glass of red wine, saying, "From your reserve," and then handed Jocelyn a glass of beer. When they ordered, Kit hesitated.

"Do you want a steak? Or seafood?" Gage asked.

"I guess a steak," Kit said.

Gage nodded. "Do the porterhouse for two, Lyonnaise potatoes and a chopped salad for each of us," she said to Tim. "Kit, you like ranch on your salad, right?"

Kit nodded. Her eyes went to the cost of the porterhouse for two, and she felt faint suddenly. Jocelyn put her arm around Kit's shoulders.

"Easy, little one. She can afford it," Jocelyn said, grinning.

"Who can afford over a hundred dollars for a steak?" Kit asked.

Jocelyn gave the girl a wink. "She can."

After the best meal Kit could remember ever having and listening to Jocelyn and Gage tell stories about their time in the Middle East, they walked out to the curb. Jocelyn surprised Gage by letting her drive. In the vehicle, Gage glanced over at Jocelyn, who'd gotten quiet suddenly. At a red light, Gage reached over and touched Jocelyn's cheek.

"You're getting a headache, aren't you?"

Jocelyn nodded, exhaling slowly. Gage grimaced.

"Okay, we'll be at the hotel in a minute. I don't suppose you have your meds with you…"

Jocelyn shook her head.

"Okay. We'll get ahead of it, Gun," Gage said, glancing back at Kit.

They got back to the hotel five minutes later. When they got out of the vehicle, Kit could see the pain on Jocelyn's face and knew this wasn't a run-of-the-mill headache. Gage hung back as Jocelyn proceeded to the elevator.

"Go to that shop they have here—grab anything with caffeine, and if they have anything for migraines, grab that too. Charge it to the room, okay?"

"Is she okay?" Kit asked as she nodded.

"She gets vicious headaches, leftovers from the crash."

"I'll be up as fast as I can," Kit said.

"Thanks." Gage strode quickly to catch up to Jocelyn, who was leaning against the window of the hotel, her head against the cold glass. "Come on, Gun, let's get you upstairs."

Jocelyn let Gage pull her gently into the elevator. Inside, she leaned against the back wall, her hands clasped tightly on the bar behind her. Gage knew that Jocelyn was fighting the urge to throw up, especially when other people got on. Gage moved to the back of the elevator and put her hand on Jocelyn's right arm, sliding it down and applying pressure to the inside of the other woman's wrist. It was an acupressure point that helped relieve nausea. Jocelyn let her breath out slowly, closing her eyes in relief at the easing of the nausea.

When they got to their floor, Gage kept her hand on Jocelyn's arm, leading her off the elevator. She noticed a number of looks, and she was sure people recognized her. She didn't care—her friend was in pain, and she needed to help fix it.

When Kit entered the room, she was surprised to see Gage sitting up on the bed with Jocelyn's body half over hers, her head against Gage's stomach. Gage's hands were in Jocelyn's hair, and Kit could see them moving rhythmically, massaging and rubbing. It was a very different scene than the one the night before, but it was obvious once again that this was something they'd done before and often.

"I got Mountain Dew because they said it has more caffeine than Coke, and I also got a Red Bull and the darkest chocolate they had—they said that's higher in caffeine too."

"It is. Perfect, Kit, thank you," Gage said. "Now if you can get me some ice, find a bag and grab a hand towel…"

"You got it." Kit left the room.

"Gun, I need you to eat some of this chocolate and guzzle this Red Bull, okay?"

Jocelyn sat up slowly. Gage moved to support her, handing her the Red Bull first; she knew Jocelyn hated the flavor, so she'd follow it up with the chocolate. Jocelyn drank the Red Bull, making a face but hurting far too much to argue. Gage opened the chocolate and broke off pieces to hand to Jocelyn, who chewed them, looking extremely pained as she did.

"Last bit, Gun. You know we need to get this in you," Gage said gently.

Jocelyn nodded as she swallowed the last bits of chocolate.

"Okay, come here." Gage pulled Jocelyn down to lay her head against Gage's torso again. She put her hands back in Jocelyn's hair, moving her hands soothingly through it and massaging her neck, feeling the knotted muscles there.

Kit walked in and handed Gage the ice in the bag and the towel.

"Thanks," Gage said, putting the towel around the ice bag and laying it against the base of Jocelyn's head.

Jocelyn jumped slightly.

"Sorry, babe. We gotta break this cycle…"

Kit stood watching as Gage held Jocelyn against her. Jocelyn's hands were clenched around the material of Gage's sweatshirt.

"Is there anything else I can do?" Kit asked softly.

Gage shook her head. "No, I just need to get her to sleep."

Kit nodded. "I'll be right out here if you need me, okay?"

"Thank you," Gage said, smiling.

Kit left the room, leaving the door open so she'd hear if Gage needed her. After about an hour, Gage emerged from the bedroom.

"Is she okay?" Kit asked from the couch.

Gage sat down on the couch with her. "Yeah, she's asleep now. This one hit fast. Usually we have more warning and can get out ahead of it."

"How often does she get them?"

"Probably four or five a month, but normally she has pain meds she can take when she feels one coming on. She just didn't have them today."

Kit nodded. "I was doing some research on migraines," she said, picking up the iPad, "and they are having a lot of success with Botox injections for migraines. Is that something you guys have ever tried?"

"Botox injections?" Gage asked, raising an eyebrow. "Gun?" She grinned. "That'd blow her mind completely."

"Well, you can read this article about them," Kit said. "Maybe she could try it."

Gage smiled at Kit. "I will read it, thank you."

Gage laid her head back against the back of the couch, closing her eyes for a moment.

"I really like Jocelyn," Kit said.

"Yeah, she's pretty cool, huh?" Gage said. "And it looks like she might be coming to work with us."

"Really?" Kit asked, surprised by the proprietary feeling she had suddenly.

"Yeah," Gage said. "I've asked her to be my chief deputy."

Kit nodded. "You said she might, though?"

"Yeah, she's thinking about it. She really hates LA, so it's kind of a major decision for her."

"But you and your son are out in LA, and I'm sure she misses you both."

"Yeah," Gage said. "That's probably what's going to win out in the end."

Gage's phone rang. She pulled it out, read the display and smiled.

"Mom," she said, answering the call. She put her booted feet up on the coffee table and bent her knees, scooting down on the couch so her back was on the seat. "Yeah, I'm actually up in San Francisco right now. Why didn't you tell me you were coming home?" She listened for a moment then laughed. "Well, surprise, I'm not there! Uh-huh, yeah, of course Jos is here… I'm at a conference. We'll be back on Thursday… Of course—just toss my shit in the downstairs suite, no big deal… Who? Oh, she's with you? Okay, no worries… Are you two, uh… you know… Oh, okay, sure, just friends. Right, like I haven't heard that one my whole life." She laughed again, shaking her head. "Okay, if you say so, Mom. But Sable Sands is fucking hot, so I'd understand if… No, no, I'm not dating anyone right now, but Sable Sands really isn't my style, Mom… Please don't tell me you brought her home with you to play matchmaker, 'cause I'll fuckin' kill ya." She laughed again. "Yeah, Mark's there, but let me warn him before you call him. He's living with his girlfriend… Oh, you heard, okay. Well, she's a bit touchy about 'family' and people invading her space." Another laugh. "Yeah, well, let's not test that theory, Mom, okay? It's good, still adjusting… No, I haven't really looked… I know, but your house is so damned big, and I need my own space… I know… okay… right… Mom… being annoying now…" she said, grinning. "Okay, I'll talk to you later… Okay, love you… bye."

"Mom?" Kit asked.

"Yeah, she apparently came home and thought she was going to surprise me… Ha, surprise! I wasn't there."

"And she brought Sable Sands home with her? The Sable Sands?"

"Yeah," Gage said. "Apparently they've been buddying around in London all this time."

"And you think she brought her home to set you up with her?" Kit asked.

"With my mother, I never know."

"Well, you could do worse than Sable Sands, that's for sure," Kit said, looking impressed.

"I don't do rock stars," Gage said. "I was around enough of them my whole life. I have no interest in them or their lifestyle."

"Yeah, but Sable Sands is like a goddess," Kit said, her eyes shining.

Gage gave Kit a surprised look. "Big fan, I take it?"

"Oh my God, yeah," Kit said, rolling her eyes dramatically.

"Well, maybe I can set you up with her." Gage winked at her.

Kit had the insane desire to say something crazy, so she clamped her mouth shut, standing up as she stretched.

"I think I'm going to head to bed," she said, glancing down at Gage. "Unless you need me for anything else…"

"No, I'm good," Gage said, her mind already elsewhere.

"Okay, goodnight," Kit said, moving past Gage.

"Goodnight," Gage said. "Hey, Kit?"

Kit turned to her boss, who was sitting on the low-slung, modern-looking white leather couch, her booted feet on the coffee table, her long red hair lying over the back of the couch. It was a striking picture.

"Yeah?" Kit asked, her voice breaking slightly on the word.

"Thanks for your help today, and tonight," Gage said, smiling warmly. "I really appreciate everything."

Kit smiled back. "Thank you for dinner. It was amazing."

"We're not even, young lady," Gage said, winking at her.

Kit shook her head. "Goodnight," she repeated.

"Goodnight."

Gage walked back into the bedroom, took off her clothes and got into the shower. Afterwards, she climbed into bed next to Jocelyn, lying on her side. She put her hand on her friend's shoulder and fell asleep with that connection between them.

Chapter 5

The morning the conference started, Gage turned over to see Jocelyn watching her. Jocelyn was sitting up, her jeans and tank top on. Her knees were bent, and her arms were draped over them.

Gage rubbed her eyes as she sat up. "What's up?"

"I'll do it," Jocelyn said, but she looked far from happy.

"Gun, I don't want you to feel like you have to."

"You asked me for help, Jock. Either you need me or you don't—which is it?"

"I need you," Gage said immediately. "But that doesn't mean—"

"Yeah, it does," Jocelyn said, cutting her off. "I'll do it. I'll plan to be in LA by the end of the week."

"Okay," Gage said. "What do you need from me?"

Jocelyn shrugged. "Place to stay till I find one."

Gage grinned. "Well, Mom's house is now filling up."

"All eight bedrooms?" Jocelyn asked. "How many executives are you taking in?"

Gage laughed. "No, not that. Mom called me last night—she came home, I guess hoping to surprise me."

"But you weren't there," Jocelyn said.

"Nope, but she brought home a friend of hers."

"Who's that?"

"Sable Sands," Gage said, rolling her eyes.

Jocelyn laughed. "And she's trying to set you up, right?"

"She claims she's not," Gage said, "but we'll see. Doesn't matter. I'm not even close to being interested."

"'Cause your assistant is damned cute…" Jocelyn said.

"Shut up, Gun," Gage said, getting up and walking into the bathroom.

The conference began that day, and Jocelyn went back to her place to pack and prepare to move to Los Angeles. She went to the PD and applied for a leave of absence, knowing full well she'd be leaving the department but trying to protect her spot, just in case. Fortunately, the captain in charge of her unit liked her enough to grant the leave.

By Tuesday night, Gage hadn't slept since Sunday night and her shoulder was driving her crazy. She texted Jocelyn asking if she had time to come by the hotel. Jocelyn showed up an hour later. Kit was worried sick about her boss; Gage had gotten to the point of not moving her right arm because she was in so much pain.

"Where's she at?" Jocelyn asked, glancing toward the bedroom.

Kit nodded, gesturing in that direction.

"You come with me," Jocelyn said, beckoning Kit. "You need to know how to deal with this when I'm not around."

"Okay," Kit said and followed Jocelyn.

Gage was lying on the bed, on her left side, wearing a black tank top and sweat pants. Kit could see she was shifting, trying to get comfortable.

"I'm here, Jock," Jocelyn said, climbing onto the bed behind Gage. Jocelyn lay against her, using her body heat to warm the joint. She reached out and touched Gage's right shoulder.

"Okay, yeah," Jocelyn said, glancing back at Kit. She pointed to one part of Gage's shoulder. "Touch this right here."

Kit stepped over and slid her hand over Gage's shoulder, feeling the huge knot in the back.

"You need to warm it up, then start working on loosening the knot. Sometimes you might actually need to relocate her shoulder, but it doesn't feel like it's out this time." She looked down at Gage. "Please tell me you brought Vicodin with you."

"Nightstand," Gage said, her voice a gasp.

Jocelyn nodded to Kit, who reached for the bottle on the nightstand and opened it. She handed one to Jocelyn, who put it into Gage's mouth. Gage swallowed it, wincing as she did.

"Okay, easy, Jock," Jocelyn said, her voice low and soothing. "Relax. You know I can't do this if you tense up on me. Breathe for me, babe... come on... breathe..." As Jocelyn talked, she massaged Gage's shoulder, moving her hands against Gage's skin. At one point she was using both hands, one on the front of Gage's shoulder and one on the back.

Kit watched as Gage started to relax; she could see the tension leaving her body. Once again she saw how well Jocelyn knew Gage. There seemed to be no end to the ways that Jocelyn was intertwined with Gage, and now she would be coming to Los Angeles with them. Kit sighed quietly to herself. It was probably for the best.

Three days later, they flew home to Los Angeles. Gage drove Kit to her apartment, insisting on carrying Kit's luggage upstairs. Kit breathed a sigh of relief that Jack wasn't home. Gage did get an opportunity to meet Caitlyn and her mother, who was at the apartment babysitting.

"Mom, this is Gage McGinnis. She's the director I work for. Gage this is my mom, Tina."

Kit's mother, an older woman with brown hair and blue eyes like Kit's, smiled warmly at Gage, extending her hand.

"It's good to meet you. Kit says you're the best thing that ever happened to the Office of Emergency Services."

Gage glanced at Kit, grinning as she took Kit's mother's hand in hers. "And Kit's making it so I can actually accomplish things without getting mired in details."

"Kit's always been very organized. I'm so glad you saw her value," Tina said.

"She's saved my life, trust me on that," Gage said, smiling.

Caitlyn came running into the room, having just gotten up from a nap. She stopped dead in her tracks when she saw the lady with the long red hair. She stared up at Gage, her blue eyes wide.

"Caitie," Kit said, "this is Gage. She's Mommy's boss. Can you say hi?"

Like she'd done with the boy in the Sierras, Gage knelt down, putting herself on eye level with the girl and extending her hand with a wide smile.

"Hi," Gage said softly to Caitlyn.

Caitlyn blinked a couple of times, putting her hand out to touch Gage's tentatively. Gage smiled again as the child's hand touched hers.

"Oh, that's pretty nail polish," Gage said, seeing the pink polish on the girl's fingertips.

"We had a nail-painting party." Tina winked at Caitlyn. "Didn't we, honey?"

Caitlyn nodded, smiling at her grandmother.

"That sounds like it was probably fun," Gage said.

"Yes," Caitlyn said, her blue eyes wide.

Kit and Tina exchanged a look. Caitlyn almost never spoke to strangers.

"Well, it's good that you had fun while I borrowed your mom for a bit, but you see? I brought her home safe and sound, okay?"

Caitlyn smiled, nodding vehemently.

"That way maybe I can borrow her again sometime, right?" Gage's green eyes stared into the girl's.

"Right," Caitlyn said, smiling brightly at Gage.

"Excellent!" Gage said, smiling too. "Well, I better get going. My mother will be climbing the walls wondering where I am." Gage stood and turned to Tina again. "It was good to meet you, ma'am," she said, extending her hand to Tina again.

Tina smiled. "You too."

"Kit, I'll see you Monday, right?" Gage asked.

"Yes, ma'am."

"That'll cost ya," Gage said, winking at Kit's use of "ma'am."

"Dang it!" Kit said, laughing.

Gage left the apartment then, running into a man coming up the stairs. He was about the same height as her, but stocky. He stared at her openmouthed for a long minute, but then moved past her. He wore blue overalls and was generally decent-looking, not that he was anything to write home about. Gage knew this was Kit's husband because his overalls had his name on them. She found herself thinking about him as she drove back to her mother's house. She could see how he might have been more attractive four years and about thirty pounds ago; still, he didn't seem good-looking enough to catch someone like Kit. Regardless, he was her husband, and she needed to deal with him in her own way. Gage just hoped Kit would be brave enough to do something about the situation she was in.

As Gage walked into the house, she could hear music pumping throughout it. She could always tell when her mother was home—music would be on constantly. Walking through the house, Gage looked around, trying to figure out where her mother was. She ran into Sable Sands first—she was in the kitchen, dancing around to the music and opening a beer. Her back was to Gage, so she didn't realize she was being observed. The song that was on had a very Middle Eastern feel to it, like belly-dance music. It was apparently what it sounded like to Sable as well, as she moved her body in a sultry belly-dance style. Gage had to hand it to the other woman; she definitely had a sexy groove to her. Sable turned around and jumped slightly.

"Oh my God, scare the life out of me, why don't you?" Sable said, smiling.

"Sorry. The music's a bit... loud." Gage gave her a pointed look.

"Sorry," Sable said, picking up the remote and turning the music down. "Your mom and I have the same taste in music, so it's very cool to have this whole-house system."

"Where is my mom?" Gage asked.

"She went upstairs to change."

"Okay, if she's gonna walk back in here half naked, tell me now," Gage said, holding up her hand. "That is something I do not need to see again in this lifetime."

Sable started to laugh. "No, your mom and I are not sleeping together."

Gage appeared unconvinced, but she nodded.

"No, seriously," Sable said, more vigorously.

Gage grinned. "Okay."

"She didn't tell me how beautiful you are though," Sable said, her warm chocolate-brown eyes widening slightly.

"Uh, yeah…" Gage said, shaking her head. "I'm not into rock stars even in the least serious sense."

Sable gazed at her, her lips pursed in thought. Gage imagined that not too many women turned her down flat. Sable's sexual prowess was legendary in the lesbian community, so most woman would kill for a chance to sleep with her. Looking at the rock star now, Gage could see the appeal. The woman was very definitely hot and oozed sex appeal from every pore. She had long chestnut-brown hair that looked smooth and sexy, and warm chocolate-brown eyes. She also had a body that most twenty-five-year-olds would kill for, and yet Sable Sands was reported to be well past that in age.

"So you don't want to think about it or anything?" Sable asked.

"No offense, really," Gage said, smiling. "You're incredibly hot and everything, but it's just not my scene."

Sable nodded slowly, licking her lips, her eyes sparkling in the sunlight coming through the windows in the kitchen.

"She turn you down already?" Lenna asked as she entered the kitchen, walking over to her daughter and hugging her.

Sable winked at Gage. "Just about as fast as you said she would."

"Nice." Gage laughed as she hugged her mother. "Was this some kind of bet?"

"We didn't put money on it or anything," Lenna said, hopping up onto the large island in the center of the kitchen. "So you were up in San Francisco, and obviously got some sleep. How are you going to sleep with Gun up there?"

"Well, she'll be here tomorrow, so…"

Lenna glanced over at Sable. "The crash I told you about—my daughter seemed to lose her ability to sleep unless she's completely exhausted. She sleeps best around her best friend and co-pilot, Gun."

"Gun?" Sable repeated.

"Her real name is Jocelyn," Gage said. "I started calling her Gun because she was my gunner, but apparently her middle name is Gunnar with an 'a,' so… go figure."

"I see," Sable said. "And you can only sleep when she's around?"

"Well, I sleep," Gage said. "I just sleep much better around her. The doctors claim it's some kind of associative thing with the crash and all. They say that I'll eventually snap out of it. Hasn't happened yet, and the crash was twelve years ago."

"And she lives in San Francisco, and you live here?" Sable asked.

"Yeah, but as of tomorrow, she lives here too." Gage grinned at her mother.

"You've actually talked her into moving to Los Angeles? You said she hates Los Angeles," Lenna said.

"She does," Gage said. "I just think she misses Mark and me more than she hates LA."

"What's she going to do for work here?" Lenna asked.

"Actually, I've asked her to come be my CDD," Gage said. "Chief deputy director," she explained when Lenna looked back at her blankly.

"And what is that, compared to you?" Lenna asked.

"She'd be my co-pilot again, my second in command."

Lenna looked thoughtful, then she shook her head. "You girls should just be a couple already, seriously."

Gage laughed. "I know you don't get it, Mom, but we're just not like that."

"You sleep together, right?" Lenna asked.

"Only when one of us needs it." Gage sighed. She'd had this conversation with her mother a thousand times. "It's not like we have sex all the time, Mom."

"But you have sex, and you're good together… Why wouldn't you be a couple?"

"Because we're not, Mom. We're just not right for each other like that—you just gotta trust me on that. Gun needs something completely different from me in a relationship."

Lenna shook her head. "What you two have is more than some lesbians ever have."

"But it's not enough for either of us, Mom," Gage said. "We both want more. We both want… perfect."

"There's no such thing," Sable said, her tone slightly sharp.

Gage looked over at Sable, surprised by her statement.

"I think there is," Gage said.

"No, there isn't," Sable said. "Trust me, I was smart and gave up on that a while ago. You should give it up before you lose what you do have."

With that Sable walked out of the kitchen. Lenna stared after her, a contemplative expression on her face, then she turned back to her daughter.

"What was that about?" Gage asked, her eyes wide.

"She had a rough breakup a while back. She's still not over it," Lenna said. "I was gonna drag her out tomorrow night for a night of fun."

Gage nodded. "Well, come down to the Club. I'd love for you to meet Jericho Tehrani and the group."

"The group?" Lenna asked. "Is this the group of women you met through Midnight?"

"Yeah, they're pretty awesome. Besides, Gun'll be here, so I was going to take her down tomorrow night too."

Lenna nodded. "Okay, sounds good. I think we'll do that. We should all go out to dinner ahead of time."

"Sounds like a plan," Gage said. "So you knew I'd turn Sable down, huh?"

"Of course I did," Lenna said, smiling. "I know my baby girl. I just keep hoping it's because you're finally going to be smart and grab ahold of Gun."

"Well, don't be holding your breath, Mom," Gage said, winking at her mother. "I'm gonna go take a shower and unpack. Are we just going to order in?"

"That's what I was thinking," Lenna said. "I noted my menu drawer gained a few extra menus…"

Gage laughed. "Gun's the cook, Mom. You know I manage to burn water."

"Yes, we're two of a kind in that respect." Lenna said. "Is Gun going to stay here at the house with us?"

"Yeah, if that's cool," Gage said. "Just till she finds a place."

"Gage Flannery McGinnis, you know that Gun is just like a daughter to me. She is welcome to stay here as long as she wants or needs."

"Okay, okay, wind your neck in. I was just asking."

"Don't you 'wind your neck in' at me, girlie," Lenna said, grinning.

***

Jocelyn drove up to the house, her car window down, her radio blaring. She'd spent a fortune on a sound system for her car, and it could be heard even from inside.

Gage was just coming downstairs when she heard the sound of P.O.D's "Boom" playing on the stereo, as well as the loud 8-liter V10 engine.

"Mom! Gun's here!" she called as she opened the front door of the house and walked out to the drive. "Jesus, how many land speed records did you break on the way here?" she asked as Jocelyn climbed out of the car.

"More than a few," Jocelyn said, grinning.

Lenna, followed by Sable, walked out of the house. Lenna hugged Jocelyn immediately, having to reach up to do so, since Jocelyn was a good six feet tall with her old brown cowboy boots on.

"How are ya, handsome?" Lenna asked, looking up at Jocelyn.

"I'm good, Mom, I'm good," Jocelyn said.

Sable observed Jocelyn from the front steps of the house. The car was a surprise, a matte Army-green Dodge Viper with a very aggressive-looking appearance package and, from the sound of the engine when she'd driven up, definitely the power to back it up. Jocelyn herself was far from what Sable had expected as well—tall, lean-framed, wearing faded jeans, caramel-brown cowboy boots, and a black tank top with a vintage-looking brown leather bomber jacket. She was definitely butch, but a very hot butch, to be sure.

"I hear you're moving down here to help this one out, huh?" Lenna said, putting her hand to Gage's shoulder.

Jocelyn smiled. "Yeah…" she said, letting her voice trail off.

"Well, come in the house. It's too damned cold out here right now," Lenna said.

They walked inside.

"When's the rest of your stuff get here?" Gage asked.

"Well, half of it's going into storage for now," Jocelyn said, reaching up to take off her jacket in the warm house. "The other half should be here in about two hours or so, depending on how long of a lunch break they charge me for."

Sable found herself watching avidly as Jocelyn removed her jacket. She realized quickly that though Jocelyn was lean, she also had muscle; her arms were well defined, but not overly large at all. She also noticed that Jocelyn's eyes had barely skipped by her. Sable wondered at that.

"Oh, sorry—Gun, this is Sable Sands." Lenna nodded toward Sable, who'd stayed out of the way.

Jocelyn's eyes were on Sable then. "I recognize her," she said in a matter-of-fact tone.

"Well, Sable, this is Gun, Jocelyn Mann. Gage's friend."

Sable nodded, a slight smile on her face.

Jocelyn and Gage exchanged a look, and Jocelyn rolled her eyes. Gage made a point of going over to the refrigerator and pulled out a beer for Jocelyn, opening it and handing it to her.

"And that's why I love you," Jocelyn said, taking the beer and draining half the bottle.

"Did you have lunch?" Lenna asked.

"Nah, but I'm good, Ma, don't worry about me. Come tell me what kind of trouble you've been into lately," Jocelyn said as she walked over to the couch.

Sable looked over at Gage. "She's rather... dynamic, huh?"

Gage grinned. "That's Gun," she said, then grabbed a beer for herself and offered Sable one; Sable accepted. They walked into the living room and sat around talking, and in Sable's case observing, for the next couple of hours.

Later that afternoon, Gage and Jocelyn were down in the game room playing pool.

"You were more than a little chilly to Sable earlier," Gage said, standing holding her pool cue.

Jocelyn was lining up her shot. Leaning far across the table, she glanced over her shoulder at Gage. "So?"

"You're still pissed about that article, aren't you?" Gage said.

"What article?" Jocelyn asked, making her shot and missing.

"What article? Who do you think you're talking to, Gun?"

Jocelyn smiled as Gage checked out the table and decided on her shot.

"It was a stupid fuckin' thing to say," Jocelyn said.

"It was five years ago, Gun, Jesus!" Gage made her shot and sank the ball.

Jocelyn shrugged. "I just don't feel like pretending I didn't read it and that it wasn't talking about me and my type."

"She wasn't talking about you," Gage said, evaluating her next shot. "She was talking about butches in general."

"Yeah, so that included you. Why doesn't it piss you off?"

"'Cause I know rock stars, Gun, and they don't always mean things that they say, or they get misquoted. It's not that big of a deal."

"She referred to us as basically men, Jock. That's not okay with me."

Gage shook her head. "You take shit far too personal, Gun, you really do." She made her shot and missed.

Jocelyn chalked her cue and moved around the table, checking out the setup of the balls and trying to figure out her shot.

"It isn't like I knocked myself out writing her hate mail or anything." Jocelyn leaned over the table to line up her shot. "I just don't like what she said, and I'm not going to pretend I like her."

"You don't know her, Gun. You know one stupid thing she said in an interview five years ago. Jesus…"

Jocelyn didn't respond; she just lined up her shot and took it, sinking the ball.

That night they went to Amarone, an Italian restaurant off Sunset Boulevard. Jocelyn wore dark blue jeans, black cowboy boots, a gray jersey with the word "Boi" on it, and a black jean jacket with a gray hoodie liner. Her belt had a picture of a helicopter and the words "AH-64 Apache" on the buckle, as well as "Gunner" in script. She wore a heavy brushed-nickel watch with a blue face, heavy silver rings, and a thick silver chain around her neck. She was all butch, that was for sure.

Sable wore black leather pants, brown leather knee-high boots, a black silk camisole, and a brown leather jacket that cut in sharply at her small waist and then flared slightly to fall just below her hips. Her makeup was as usual done in shades of gold to bring out the gold flecks in her chocolate-brown eyes; her lips were a tawny color, matching the shade of her blush. Her long chestnut-brown hair, shot through with highlights of copper and lowlights of rich auburn, was loose and falling in sexy soft waves down her back.

Lenna had opted for a simple black-and-green peasant-style dress with thigh-high black leather boots and a long black suede coat. Gage was dressed in a black button-up shirt, jeans, black boots, and a black biker jacket, and her red hair was loose and straight.

At the restaurant, Gage and Jocelyn had a lively discussion about why Gage refused to try anything "different."

"It's just cheese, tomatoes and olive oil, Jock—just try it," Jocelyn said, holding out a piece of cheese and tomato.

"Jos, I prefer that kind of stuff on my pizza, thanks." Gage sat back with her arms folded in front of her chest.

"It's good," Sable put in, taking some and dipping it in the olive oil on the plate.

Jocelyn looked at Sable, the look measuring, then back at Gage.

"Just try it," she said.

"No," Gage said simply, her green eyes sparkling in humor.

"But if I go back there and melt it on a piece of bread you'll eat it?" Jocelyn's tone indicated how crazy that was.

"Yep," Gage said.

Jocelyn shook her head. "Junk-food junkie, I'm telling you…"

"And damned proud of it," Gage said.

"So I'm betting I can guess what you're going to order," Jocelyn said.

"Yep, the steak and potatoes."

"And you're gonna do the same thing, aren't you, Mom?" Jocelyn said to Lenna.

Lenna laughed, nodding.

"It's no wonder she eats like she does," Jocelyn said.

"I take all the blame," Lenna said with a laugh.

Jocelyn was pleasantly, if silently, impressed when Sable ordered not only the linguine and clams but also striped bass for dinner, and did so in perfectly accented Italian as well.

"Jocelyn, would you share the seafood risotto with me? I want to try it, but I can't eat all of that," Sable said, glancing over at Jocelyn.

"No one calls me Jocelyn, not even my mother," Jocelyn said as she nodded to the waiter who was waiting to take their order. "I'll have the strozzapreti and shrimp, and the veal and mushroom. And add the risotto for the lady, too, please."

When the waiter walked away, Sable looked at Jocelyn. "Gage calls you Jos," she pointed out.

"Gage is the only one that gets away with it," Jocelyn countered. "And even that isn't my full name."

"What does your mother call you?" Sable asked.

"She doesn't," Jocelyn replied in a voice that indicated that the discussion was closed.

Sable glanced at Gage and saw that she and Lenna were grimacing slightly at each other. She knew then that she'd hit a sore subject. She turned back to Jocelyn again; the woman was looking at her, as if waiting for her to say something else stupid. Sable lowered her eyes. She hadn't meant to hurt anyone's feelings.

Later the four entered the bar, and there was instant reaction to the fact that not only was Lenna McGinnis there but so was Sable Sands—the lesbians were all in an uproar. While Sable and Lenna handled their many fans, Gage took Jocelyn over to meet the group. When they got there, however, there was a very definite sense of tension.

"What's going on?" Gage asked Jericho.

"Sable Sands being here isn't a good thing," Jericho said. "She knows your mother?"

"Yeah, they've been palling around in London together. Why is Sable being here bad?"

"Because she's my ex," Cat said, walking up. "She's here with you, Gage?"

"Well, she's here with us," Gage said, gesturing to her mother and then to Jocelyn. "Cat, this is Gun. She's my best friend."

"Nice to meet you." Cat smiled, her eyes flicking from Jocelyn to Sable working the crowd.

"So she probably doesn't even know you're here," Jovina said to Cat.

"It's not going to keep her from causing drama, Jovi," Cat said, shaking her head.

"She'll behave herself or we'll leave," Jocelyn said, her voice strong.

Cat took in Jocelyn's dark eyes and the set of her jaw. She nodded to the other woman. "Okay."

As Sable made her way over to where Gage and Jocelyn had walked to, she saw Catalina and stopped dead in her tracks. Her eyes moved over the other women and located Jovina standing a couple of feet from Catalina. So they were still together? There was the slightest flash of sadness in her eyes before the mask of confidence fell. Jocelyn saw it and wished she hadn't, because her gallant streak kicked in then.

Walking over to the group, Sable nodded to the women as Gage made introductions. Sable naturally recognized the other two rock stars, Xandy and Wynter; she smiled at them. Sable's eyes kept straying over to Catalina and Jovina, and she could see that Catalina was watching her closely, as if trying to determine her intent.

To Sable's shock, Jocelyn casually walked over to stand behind her, leaned down and whispered, "What do you need to drink?"

Sable glanced up at Jocelyn gratefully. "Double shot of tequila, please."

"Got it," Jocelyn said. "Gage, beer?"

Gage nodded.

"Mom, Glenlivet?" Jocelyn asked.

"Yes, love, thank you," Lenna said.

After all the introductions were made, Catalina walked over to Sable.

"What are you doing here?" she asked, her tone all cop.

"Visiting with my friends," Sable replied airily.

"And you didn't know we were here?"

"How would I know where you and she hang out, Catalina? I'm not psychic."

"I know you, Sable," Cat said, narrowing her eyes, "and I know you have a lot of connections in the community, so do me a favor and don't treat me like I'm an idiot, okay?"

Jocelyn had returned by this time and walked up to stand behind Catalina.

"Do me a favor and back up off the lady, okay?" Jocelyn said, her tone friendly but her eyes quite serious.

Cat glanced up at Jocelyn, since Jocelyn was a good half a foot taller than she was.

Jocelyn looked back at Cat, her expression indicating she had no intention of backing down. Finally, Cat put her hands up in a surrendering gesture and walked away after giving Sable a pointed look. Jocelyn handed Sable the shot, which she took gratefully. Jocelyn handed Gage and Lenna their drinks as well.

"Where's yours?" Gage asked.

"Not enough hands." Jocelyn gestured to a waitress passing by. The waitress walked over to Jocelyn immediately, smiling up at her sexily. "Can I get a Captain and Coke, with an extra shot?"

"Of course."

"Thanks," Jocelyn said, winking at the girl.

Sable had drunk the shot and handed the glass to the waitress. The girl smiled brightly at Sable.

"Can I bring you anything else, Miss Sands?"

"Yes, another one of those," Sable said. "Double shot of tequila."

"You got it."

When the waitress walked away, Sable turned to Jocelyn, catching the taller woman's eyes. She nodded; Jocelyn inclined her head.

Later, Jocelyn leaned against one of the tables, her eyes roving over the group. She wasn't as social as Gage; she tended to keep to herself until she knew the lay of the land. Gage glanced over at her friend a few times, but she knew Jocelyn well enough to know how she was, so she didn't bug her. Jocelyn noted Catalina talking to her girlfriend, their eyes often straying over to Sable.

At one point Cat walked over to Sable. Jocelyn noted that Sable tensed when she saw Cat approaching. Jocelyn watched them talk and Cat gesture to the back patio; she found it necessary to follow, reaching into her pocket for her cigarettes as she did. Cat and Sable walked toward a side table. Jocelyn followed but stayed five feet from them. Lighting her cigarette, she paced slowly, meandering in circles that kept her close to the two talking.

"Sable, where's Jake?" Cat glanced up to see Jocelyn keeping tabs on them.

"He's in Ireland. His mother died," Sable said sadly.

"Oh, God," Cat said. "Please tell him how sorry I am."

"I will."

"So what are you doing for a bodyguard in the meantime?" Cat asked.

"I'm not really doing anything. I told Jake I'd find someone..." Sable said.

"He'd kill you if he knew you'd been out like this without anyone guarding you."

"I know," Sable said, her look serious; her bodyguard was pretty fierce about her being protected at all times.

Cat glanced at Jocelyn again. "You know you could just come sit down," she said, her tone even.

"I'm good," Jocelyn answered simply.

"Looks like you've got a self-appointed bodyguard already," Cat said.

"The funny thing is, I don't think she even likes me," Sable whispered to Cat.

"How is that even possible?" Cat asked sarcastically.

"I know, right?" Sable put her hand over Cat's on the table. "I really had no idea you would be here, I swear."

Cat looked over at Jocelyn again, more intently this time. "Okay, you're making me nervous doing that. Could you please just sit down?"

"The point is to make people nervous," Jocelyn said.

Cat narrowed her eyes at Jocelyn and received the same look in return.

Cat looked back at Sable, shrugging.

"I guess I tend to assign you superpowers sometimes," Cat said, smiling.

"The power of omniscience?" Sable asked.

"Yeah," Cat said, rolling her eyes.

"I see you two are still together," Sable said, doing her best to keep the haunted sound out of her voice but not totally succeeding. Even Jocelyn heard it.

Cat nodded. "We're the real deal, Sable. I tried to tell you that before…"

"I know, I just wasn't ready to hear it," Sable said. "I still don't think I am."

Cat took a deep breath. "I just can't have you trying anything, okay? I won't risk my relationship with her to be gentle on you."

"I won't try anything, Cat. I'm not really that into rejection."

Cat chuckled softly. "You know I love you," she said. "I'm just in love with Jovi."

Sable nodded, not trusting her voice to speak. She'd known that Catalina wasn't in love with her. If she had been, she'd have stayed with her, but Catalina had still been hung up on Elizabeth Endicott at the time.

"I'm going to head back inside. You're okay out here?" Cat asked, glancing over at Jocelyn

"Yeah." Sable said.

Cat stood up and walked inside. Sable sat back, blowing her breath out.

Jocelyn walked over and handed Sable a double shot of tequila she'd gotten from the outside bar. Sable took the shot and drank it quickly, nodding to Jocelyn.

"Thanks," she said.

Jocelyn sat down in the chair Cat had just left. She didn't say anything, just sat with Sable, smoking and waiting for her to gather herself together. After a few minutes, Sable stood up.

"I need to dance," Sable said. "Do you dance?"

"I've been accused of it a couple of times," Jocelyn answered mildly.

"Will you come dance with me?" Sable looked so openly terrified of rejection that there was no way Jocelyn could say no.

Jocelyn took Sable's hand and led her inside and to the dance floor. They danced for a number of songs. Jocelyn could see that the shots Sable had drunk were definitely hitting her. When they finally left the dance floor, Jocelyn steered Sable toward the bar. She ordered another shot for herself and a Captain and Coke, then ordered a single shot for Sable. When the drinks came, Jocelyn pulled out two twenties and handed them to the bartender.

"I can pay for the drinks…" Sable started to say.

"Not with me you can't," Jocelyn said, matter of fact.

Jocelyn wouldn't really even look at her. Sable had no idea what to make of Jocelyn's actions now versus the way she'd been acting toward her earlier. On the one hand, it appeared to Sable that Jocelyn didn't really like her, but then she'd been a strong presence all evening at the bar. It made no sense to her at all.

Gage spent the evening with her mother, watching others dance. She'd been surprised at first by Jocelyn's actions with Sable, but then she realized her friend was being her usual gallant self. Even if she didn't like Sable, Jocelyn wouldn't let a woman be harassed or treated badly. Cat had calmed down after talking to Sable. Gage watched Cat and Jovina talking, laughing and occasionally kissing. She also watched couples like Jericho and Zoey, Devin and Skyler, and Rayden and Gray. It made her feel melancholy for that other half. Normally she would have hung with Jocelyn, but even that wasn't an option. Jocelyn seemed to be purposely keeping Sable away from the rest of the group. Gage understood it, but it didn't make her any less depressed.

Later that night when they got back to the house, Gage did her best to go to sleep. She failed miserably and ended up going downstairs to the room Jocelyn was in, just off the game room. She didn't notice Sable sitting in one of the chairs in the game room's corner. Gage walked into Jocelyn's room, not closing the door all the way.

She went over to the bed, climbing onto it and straight into Jocelyn's arms.

"Whoa," Jocelyn said, wrapping her arms around Gage as her partner snuggled against her almost desperately. "What's goin' on, Jock?"

Gage shook her head, moving to Jocelyn's side, her hands sliding under the tank top she wore to touch bare skin.

Jocelyn jumped and gasped at the contact. Gage wasn't usually this aggressive unless she was really wound up. Jocelyn knew better than to ask too many questions. She leaned in to kiss Gage; her lips were met hungrily with Gage's.

Within minutes they were both crying out loudly in their release. They lay together trying to catch their breath, both naked. Gage fell asleep against Jocelyn, her left hand on Jocelyn's shoulder possessively. Jocelyn lay half sitting up. She still wasn't sure what had instigated the visit, but she knew it had obviously been what Gage had needed. Still lying with Gage against her, one long leg stretched out and one arm behind her head, Jocelyn was lost in thought. She caught movement by the door and lifted her head to see Sable looking at her.

Sable had heard Gage and Jocelyn's lovemaking, and even though she knew she should leave, she'd been drawn to the partially open door by an insatiable curiosity. As she peeked into the room, she saw Gage lying against Jocelyn. Her gaze traveled over all the skin on display, then her eyes reached Jocelyn's, and she saw that Jocelyn was staring back at her. She also saw the sardonic grin that curled Jocelyn's lips.

For some reason, Jocelyn was not surprised to see Sable standing at the door to the room. In some insane way, it excited her to know that Sable had probably heard her and Gage minutes before. She smiled wickedly as she bent her knee to place her foot flat on the bed, her expression changing to one of open amazement that Sable was continuing to stare.

Sable pursed her lips, seeing the look on Jocelyn's face and wanting to shock her further, but she decided she'd best just back down. She eased out of the doorway and turned and left the room. She had a really hard time getting to sleep that night, and she was even more confused by Gage and Jocelyn's relationship. She was also more confused about Jocelyn Mann.

The next morning, Jocelyn woke to find Gage looking up at her. She immediately recognized the look and started shaking her head.

"We've been through this…" Jocelyn sighed.

"I know, but explain it to me again," Gage said. "Why can't we be a couple?"

"Because it doesn't work, Jock," Jocelyn said. "Because you need someone to need you… and I don't need anyone, not like you need me to."

"You think that's what it is," Gage said.

"Gage, seriously," Jocelyn said. "You love all that hero shit. You want to be the knight in shining armor riding in with colors flying. I'm not someone that needs rescuing, and when we try a relationship you get bored, you get antsy, and we fight like cats and dogs. I love you, but I'm not the person you're meant for."

Gage sighed. "I know, I just… I hate this."

"Believe me, babe—if I could change who I am to be what you need, I'd do it. But you don't grow up half raising seven brothers and sisters being needy, trust me."

"Maybe I can change," Gage said, her face hopeful.

"You shouldn't have to, Gage," Jocelyn said. "The whole point of being with the person you were meant for means that you get to be exactly who you are with them. If you change to be with me, then you aren't you anymore."

"You suck," Gage said petulantly.

"I know," Jocelyn said with a grin.

"And I hate you."

"I know that too."

"And you're lousy in bed," Gage said.

"Hey, now you're just being mean."

Gage put her hand to Jocelyn's cheek. "I love you, and you are the best friend I have…"

"Now you're just trying to make up," Jocelyn said, winking at her.

"And you love me too, even though I drag you into my shit all the time."

"It does seem that I'm the one that needs to rescue you this time, doesn't it?" Jocelyn said, not sounding unhappy at that thought.

"Yeah, and you're the only one that's allowed to rescue me." Gage kissed Jocelyn's lips.

"Good, then I'm useful," Jocelyn said, winking again. "Trust me, babe, it'll happen when it's meant to happen."

Gage moved to get out of bed. "Yeah, yeah."

"At least you're getting sleep," Jocelyn said.

"There is that." Gage said, smiling.

Chapter 6

Later that day, Jocelyn found herself stuck in a car with Sable. She wasn't sure why Fate was shoving her with this woman, but she was getting to the point of wanting to kick Fate's ass.

Gage had gone into the office, and Lenna had a meeting with her agent that was scheduled at the last minute.

"I need you to pick up my car from the shop... Can you please, Gun?" Lenna asked, her tone pleading. "Oh, crap, and I promised Sable I'd take her over to the Beverly Center. Can you do that too?"

"Do you have any dry cleaning you need picked up? Or your dog walked?" Jocelyn asked wryly.

"What?" Lenna asked. "Oh, stop being a smartass. I can drop you two off at the shop on my way to the agent's office."

"Fine," Jocelyn sighed.

An hour later, Jocelyn got onto the freeway, driving Lenna's Mercedes and cussing at it.

"Jesus, Mom, next time get a car with balls," Jocelyn muttered.

"Why do you call Lenna 'Mom'?" Sable asked.

Jocelyn glanced over at Sable hesitantly; finally she shrugged. "Because she's been more of a mother to me than my own has been for the last so many years."

Sable looked surprised. "How many?"

"Almost twenty now, for as long as I've known Gage."

"Your family doesn't accept who you are?"

"They think being gay is a disease," Jocelyn said.

"That's ridiculous."

"Is it?" Jocelyn asked, as one dark eyebrow rose.

"Of course it is," Sable said, appalled.

"I guess it's easy to lump things you don't understand together."

"What does that mean?"

"Well, you've done it," Jocelyn said.

"I have? When?"

"An article in *Outword* a while back."

"What did I say?" Sable asked, perplexed.

"Oh, let's see…" Jocelyn looked heavenward. "Something like you don't date butches because if you wanted to date men, you'd just date your bodyguard, Jake."

"Sounds to me like you know exactly what I said."

"Ya think?"

"I was half joking, you know," Sable said.

"It wasn't funny, you know," Jocelyn countered, her eyes sparkling with barely contained malice.

"So why does it bother you?"

"Are you seriously asking me that?"

"Well, I wasn't talking about you," Sable said.

"No, you were talking about my type," Jocelyn said. "And stereotyping the shit out of my type."

"I was speaking from my own experience," Sable pointed out.

"Yeah, and you made sure that your obviously limited experience was reported nationwide," Jocelyn said, her tone acerbic.

"Obviously limited experience?"

"How many butches have you dated?" Jocelyn asked.

"I-I…" Sable stammered. "Well…"

"It's a simple question."

"A couple," Sable said. "But I've known a lot of butches."

"Knowing and dating are two different things, Sable."

"Okay, let me ask you a question here," Sable said, putting her hand out to halt the diatribe that she felt coming. "Let's say that you and I were dating."

"So we're in complete fantasy land now?"

Sable gave her a foul look. "Sure, let's say that."

Sable's ego was certainly taking a beating on this trip to Los Angeles, between Gage turning her down, Cat being in love with her girlfriend, and now Jocelyn apparently not interested in her either.

"Anyway," Sable said pointedly, "so this situation, driving and all. Would you always drive?"

Jocelyn looked over at her, perplexed. "That would depend."

"On?"

"Well, is it my car or your car?"

"Let's say it's my car," Sable said.

"Okay, and do you know the area better than me, or do I know it better?" Jocelyn asked.

"Let's say I know it better."

"Then if you wanted to drive, I'd let you drive."

"Hmm," Sable said. "See? That's not my experience."

"Then you dated the wrong butches," Jocelyn said. "Still didn't give you the right to talk shit about all of us."

"Oh my God!" Sable said, throwing her hands up. "I didn't realize that I was denigrating an entire cross section. I was talking about my preferences, for God's fucking sake!"

Jocelyn raised an eyebrow at Sable, blinking a couple of times, a slight smile playing at her lips.

Sable's expression changed. "How about you let me make it up to you?"

"Why would you want to do that?" Jocelyn asked.

"Because I've obviously wronged you in some insane way, and you were really nice to me last night, so now I feel bad."

Jocelyn shook her head. "Won't erase what you said."

"Nothing will erase what I said, but maybe if I get to know a different kind of butch, the 'right kind,' then next time someone asks me about butches, I'll have some good frame of reference. Think of it as your Sable Sands improvement project."

"I wasn't aware I needed a project."

"Well, too bad. You skewered me, now you have to help fix me," Sable said in a haughty voice.

"I do not," Jocelyn said, sounding appalled.

"So you want me to just feel really awful and sad," Sable said, her look aghast.

Jocelyn pursed her lips. "You're so full of shit right now, it's not even funny."

Sable started laughing then, and it was a very contagious sound. Eventually Jocelyn was grinning too.

"I did have you going for a minute there," Sable said.

"Maybe," Jocelyn conceded. "Maybe you should have been an actress instead of a singer."

"Maybe," Sable said.

Jocelyn's phone rang then, and she answered it through the Mercedes' Bluetooth.

"Hello?"

"Mom J?" Mark queried.

"Hey, baby boy, what's up?" Jocelyn said, smiling.

"You're in town and you don't even call me?" Mark complained.

"I was going to call you, but your grandmother has me doing chauffeur duties."

"Well, when can we get together?" Mark asked. "I want you to meet Jenny."

Jocelyn grimaced, dreading that meeting, from what Gage had told her about the girl. "How about we have dinner over at Grandma's house tomorrow? I'll cook."

Sable looked at Jocelyn, shocked.

"That would be cool," Mark said. "I want Jenny to meet Grandma too."

"Well, let's say seven, okay?"

"Sounds good. We'll see you then. Love you!"

"Love you too."

They hung up then.

"You have a son?" Sable asked.

"Technically he's Gage's son," Jocelyn said, "but I helped raise him since he was ten."

"What exactly is the deal between you and Gage?" Sable asked with a questioning look.

"You mean besides the sex?" Jocelyn asked pointedly.

Sable bit her lip, looking contrite. "I'm sorry. That was really not appropriate last night. I just... I was curious. I can't figure you two out."

"And you have to figure everything out?"

Sable realized that for some reason she did want to figure Jocelyn out. She remembered feeling that way before, with Catalina Roché. It dragged at her, but she nodded to Jocelyn.

Jocelyn's look flickered, seeing something in Sable's eyes and wondering at it, but then she shrugged.

"We're friends."

"Friends?" Sable repeated.

"Yeah, with benefits, obviously," Jocelyn said, grinning.

"Obviously," Sable said. "But you two seem so close…"

"We've been friends for almost twenty years, Sable, and we've been through some serious shit together. That's going to make people close."

"But even Lenna doesn't understand why you're not a couple."

"Hell, Gage and I don't always understand it," Jocelyn said.

Sable nodded, thinking that she had a talent for being interested in complicated women.

The next day, Sable walked into the kitchen to see Jocelyn standing at the huge island in the center of the kitchen, chopping vegetables. Music was on; 3 Doors Down's "Citizen/Soldier" was playing, and Jocelyn was singing the words. One verse struck a chord with Sable; it talked about how the strongest people didn't always wear crowns.

"That song seems to fit you," Sable commented.

Jocelyn looked at her, not having noticed her in the kitchen before that.

"I like it," Jocelyn said, shrugging.

"So you cook too."

"Someone around here has to," Jocelyn said, grinning. "Neither Gage nor Lenna do. Do you?"

"Sorry," Sable said. "I'm an order-takeout kind of girl too."

Jocelyn shook her head. "It's a lost art," she said with a smile.

Sable leaned against the counter next to where Jocelyn stood. "So how come you know how to cook?"

"I had seven younger brother and sisters," Jocelyn said. "And parents who worked two jobs each, so I was in charge a lot."

"Wow, seven brothers and sisters? That's crazy."

"I take it you didn't have that many?"

"No," Sable said. "I was an only child, like Gage."

"Lucky you," Jocelyn said.

"So you said your parents don't approve of you being gay. When did you come out to them?"

"I didn't come out to them. They basically caught me with a girl."

"Oh, crap," Sable said.

"Their own fault. I was home on leave but had purposely taken a hotel room across town. My mother and father decided to come see me... Well, I had Gage with me, and we were, ah, indisposed when they showed up."

"Oh, my..." Sable said.

"It is what it is," Jocelyn said. "They'd have found out eventually. I'm not much into hiding."

"So when did you figure out you were gay?"

"In the Army, with Gage," Jocelyn said. "I'd always been a tomboy, but when I met Gage she was about as openly gay as someone could be during DADT, and I was so completely attracted there was no getting around it."

"I get that. She's pretty hot."

Jocelyn nodded, giving Sable an expectant look.

"What?" Sable asked as she picked up a carrot and popped it in her mouth.

"Nothin'," Jocelyn drawled.

"You think I'm into Gage?" Sable asked curiously.

Jocelyn shrugged. "None of my business."

"And what if I was?" Sable folded her arms in front of her chest, her head canted.

"I'd say give it a shot," Jocelyn said. "But she doesn't usually date rock stars."

"Goddamn, you do know her, don't you? That's exactly what she told me," Sable said, shaking her head. "So you're okay when she sees other women?"

"Yeah, I would be, if she ever did."

"What does that mean?" Sable asked.

"Gage hasn't really seriously dated in the entire time I've known her. She hides out with work and Mark to keep her busy."

"And has sex with you," Sable added pointedly.

"And that."

"Do you date other women?"

"I do," Jocelyn said.

"And how do they feel about your relationship with Gage?" Sable asked, getting to the root of what she was curious about.

Jocelyn looked contemplative for a moment, then shrugged. "They either get it or they don't."

"And if they don't?"

"They aren't around for long," Jocelyn said simply.

"And you think that's healthy?" Sable said.

"Healthy?" Jocelyn repeated derisively. "What's healthy? I mean, who's to say how things are supposed to be to make things 'right'?"

"I'd think it would make it fairly hard to find love," Sable said.

"Well, I've never been in love."

"Not even with Gage?"

"I love Gage," Jocelyn said, "but I'm not in love with her."

"I've never understood the difference between those two phrases," Sable said, shaking her head.

"Well, to me, loving someone means you care about them and worry about them and try to do what you can to make them happy. Being in love with someone means you'd do anything on earth to make them yours and keep them happy."

Sable was surprised by Jocelyn's statement, and it showed on her face.

"What?" Jocelyn asked. "You didn't think butches felt like that?"

Sable gave her a dirty look. "Will you quit that?" she asked. "I don't judge everyone on their appearance, Jesus! I'm just surprised to hear it put that way. I've never really thought of it like that."

"It's just my perspective. Nothing says it's right."

"But like you said, what is 'right' anyway?" Sable said.

"There you go," Jocelyn said, smiling softly.

Dinner that evening was fairly stifled and uncomfortable for everyone. Mark's girlfriend was far from friendly and seemed only interested in talking to Lenna and Sable Sands. Jocelyn and Gage exchanged looks. Even Mark seemed really uncomfortable. In the kitchen, cleaning up after Mark and Jenny left, Gage and Jocelyn were discussing their son. Lenna and Sable were sitting in the dining room and could hear the discussion.

"I don't trust her," Jocelyn was saying. "Is he even sure that kid is his?"

"Gun!" Gage said, shocked. "I'm sure he's thought about that."

"Are you?" Jocelyn asked. "You know that kid is as naive and trusting at they come."

"Despite everything you taught him, huh?" Gage asked.

"Don't make me smack you in your own mother's kitchen…"

"Yeah, yeah," Gage said, rolling her eyes. "We can't ask him about that, Gun. If he doesn't think we like her…"

"How the fuck could we like her? She didn't say five words to us!" Jocelyn exclaimed.

"I know." Gage shook her head. "That has got to be the most uncomfortable meal I've had since that first time… you know…"

"Oh fuck, don't bring that up!" Jocelyn said, laughing. "I've never been so friggin' frustrated in my entire life, and that was the longest meal ever!"

Gage laughed. "Believe it or not it was rough on me too."

"Bullshit," Jocelyn said. "You're the one that put me in that state, and then casually walked off to chow. I could have just killed ya then and saved myself a lot of grief."

"Ah, but then you wouldn't have me around now to harass you."

"True," Jocelyn said. "Life would be less entertaining, that's for sure."

"Uh-huh," Gage agreed.

Later that night, Jocelyn went for a run to try to get rid of some of the tension she was feeling. Walking back into the house, she removed her jacket, which was soaked, to reveal the black-and-gray jog bra she wore. She stopped in the kitchen to get a bottle of water and turned around at the sound of a low whistle. Sable stood leaning against the doorway from the living room to the kitchen.

"Wow," Sable said, seeing Jocelyn's cut abs, watching her arms flex as she lifted the bottle of water to her lips again. "Nice," she added, her eyes sparkling.

"Uh-huh," Jocelyn said with a wry grin.

"You really shouldn't walk around the house like that," Sable admonished.

"Why not?" Jocelyn asked, a challenge in her voice.

Sable's eyes went from Jocelyn's eyes down to her bare stomach, and then down to the slim hips encased in black yoga pants that were rather well fitted. Then she met Jocelyn's eyes again.

"It might give someone ideas…"

Jocelyn looked back at Sable, her gaze challenging as she leaned against the center island, facing her.

"What kinds of ideas?"

Sable felt her body react to the very direct come-on in Jocelyn's eyes. She felt her breath quicken and saw the slight widening of Jocelyn's dark eyes as she recognized the sign of excitement in Sable's. Without another word, Jocelyn put the bottle of water down and walked over to where Sable stood. Her lips captured Sable's as she stepped up to her.

Sable started to pull back, out of sheer surprise and what she considered some kind of natural self-preservation instinct, but Jocelyn's arm slid around her waist, dragging her closer and holding her fast as she deepened the kiss. Moaning deep in her throat, Sable felt her entire body come alive at the sheer sexuality of the situation.

When their lips parted, Jocelyn smiled smugly, her eyes reflecting her confidence that she'd just excited Sable beyond words. She then stepped back, walked over to pick up her water, and left the room. Sable walked into the kitchen and leaned her elbows on the island, doing her best to get her heartbeat under control.

That night, Jocelyn lay in bed asleep. She was awoken by the feel of a woman's naked body sliding down over hers. She moaned out loud before even waking fully. When she did wake, she fastened her lips to the pair that hovered over hers. She knew it was Sable; she recognized the sexy scent of the woman. Putting her hands to Sable's hips, she pulled her against her, grinding her pelvis against Sable's, making Sable gasp against her mouth. Jocelyn's lips were aggressive and hungry against Sable's, and Sable was responding to that demand.

The first orgasm shocked Sable to her core. She wasn't used to any woman being able to make her come that easily without even having her hand between her legs. She rode the wave of the orgasm, pressing her body against Jocelyn's desperately. As the first wave passed, Sable found herself under Jocelyn, and Jocelyn's body moved against her, pressing, moving, grinding, and Sable felt her body respond immediately. She grasped at Jocelyn's back as she came again, her body writhing under Jocelyn's.

Jocelyn's lips found hers again, kissing her deeply. As she shifted to the side, Jocelyn slid her hand over Sable's smooth skin appreciatively.

"Jesus, you have the most incredible body," Jocelyn murmured as her fingers rubbed over a hard nipple, making Sable moan again.

Sable didn't have time to respond because Jocelyn's lips were on hers again, as Jocelyn's hand slid over her skin, exciting her all over again. Sable quickly found herself begging for the first time in many years.

"Please, Gun… Please…" She moaned, wanting Jocelyn's hand to slide lower, to touch her, wanting that pressure against her wetness.

"What do you want?" Jocelyn asked, her lips at Sable's ears, so husky and low it made Sable shudder.

"Touch me," Sable begged.

Jocelyn's hand slid down, brushing past pubic hair and making Sable moan and buck. Sable felt fingers on the inside of her thigh, the heat of them seeming to radiate, and she held her breath, willing those fingers to slide upward. Jocelyn took her time, letting her thumb brush upward to touch the sensitive skin just below Sable's pussy.

"God!" Sable exclaimed, her body trembling with need.

Jocelyn moved her mouth to Sable's neck, kissing, biting and sucking at the skin there and feeling Sable's body straining against her.

"Gun, please," Sable moaned again. "I need you... I need you... please..."

Jocelyn sucked hard at the skin at the nape of Sable's neck as she slid her thumb between the lips of Sable's pussy. She felt the wetness and heat there, actually moaning herself at how good it felt to know that Sable was that excited. Sable came instantly—the combination of Jocelyn's mouth, wet and warm, sucking at her skin, the vibration of her moan, and her thumb against her hardened clit was all she could take. She felt her nails cut into Jocelyn's shoulder, but she couldn't help herself. She was coming so hard she couldn't control any part of her body. She screamed herself hoarse, even as Jocelyn tried to kiss her to keep her quiet.

Afterwards, Sable lay against Jocelyn, feeling like her entire body was still a live wire. Jocelyn lay on her side, her hand possessively on Sable's stomach, her other arm under Sable's neck and her head against the side of Sable's. When Sable managed to regain her faculties, she glanced up at Jocelyn, meeting her eyes and smiling softly.

"That was..." Sable couldn't find adequate words to describe how it had felt. No one, not even Catalina, had excited her that much.

"Uh-huh," Jocelyn murmured, her hand flexing on Sable's stomach. "And I'm not even close to being done with you yet..." she said, her voice so sexy and husky Sable felt her body respond instantly.

Three hours and an indefinable number of orgasms later, Sable finally got some of her own back when she pushed Jocelyn to her back and slid her body down over hers.

Jocelyn groaned. She hadn't come yet, having been enjoying making Sable come in every way imaginable. The feel of Sable sliding slickly over her was enough to get her body humming excitedly. She wasn't surprised that Sable was able to arouse her; the woman had a body that could excite a dead woman. However, it was a surprise when Sable took complete charge and brought her expertly to not one but three climaxes in a row.

After the third orgasm, Jocelyn used what little strength she had left to shift Sable to her side. She too rolled to her side to pull Sable against her, holding her close as Jocelyn did her best to catch her breath.

"Jesus, that was amazing," Jocelyn said breathlessly.

"You're telling me," Sable said. "I can see why Gage holds on to you with both hands."

Jocelyn chuckled. "It isn't like this with Gage."

"It isn't?" Sable asked, shocked.

Jocelyn shook her head. "No, with Gage and me it's simply the release, not the build-up, not the seduction. We both know what we're after, and we get straight to it."

Sable knew it should bother her that she liked hearing that so much, that she'd just gotten something from Jocelyn that Gage didn't get. Sable knew she was getting drawn in to Jocelyn, and she had been since she'd laid eyes on the woman. The part of her that was still getting over Catalina wanted to run and hide, but her body, pressed along the length of Jocelyn's, refused to listen to that other part.

Sable looked up at Jocelyn. "So are you done with me now?" she asked softly.

Jocelyn pulled back, her eyes searching Sable's because she sensed a hidden meaning in the question. Leaning down, she kissed Sable's lips.

"For tonight," she said, her voice intimate and soft. "But you're not going anywhere." She tightened her arms around Sable.

"Who said I wanted to go anywhere?" Sable lowered her head to kiss Jocelyn's shoulder, then put her head against that same shoulder, sighing contentedly.

Jocelyn was surprised at how good it made her feel to have Sable in her arms. She knew some of what had happened between them was her getting a little of her own back for butches everywhere, but it had changed somewhere along the way. She'd wanted to feel Sable's response to her, and she'd wanted to make her respond more. Now, lying with Sable against her, she liked the way Sable's long hair lay around her and over her arm.

They both fell asleep feeling happy and sated.

Sable woke first the next morning, looking at Jocelyn and finding that even asleep the woman was sexy as hell. Jocelyn had moved to her back, her left arm still under Sable's neck and her arm bent, her hand at Sable's back to hold her against her side. Sable's eyes roamed over Jocelyn's lips, which had been so strong and insistent on hers the night before. Her lips tingled at the thought. She touched Jocelyn's lips, running her finger over them lightly. Jocelyn stirred but didn't wake. Sable found that she desperately wanted Jocelyn to wake up the "right" way.

Lying over Jocelyn, Sable began kissing her shoulder, moving to kiss nipples that were hard in the morning chill, her hands caressing shoulders, arms and chest as she continued to kiss Jocelyn's warm skin. Suddenly Jocelyn's hands were in Sable's long hair, guiding her head, and Jocelyn moaned softly and gasped as lips contacted sensitive skin. Sable moved down further, her mouth moving, her tongue sliding over Jocelyn's pelvis.

When she was between Jocelyn's legs, she looked up at the other woman seductively. She could see the heat burning in Jocelyn's eyes as she looked back. She could also see Jocelyn's chest rising and falling with her heavy breathing.

"What do you want?" Sable asked, repeating Jocelyn's question from the night before.

"You," Jocelyn said simply.

The word ricocheted around in Sable's head, and she lowered her mouth to Jocelyn's pussy, making her come quickly and hard. Then Jocelyn's hands were at her shoulders, pulling her up, her lips capturing Sable's hungrily. They made love feverishly then, and both cried out in their mutual release. They lay together afterwards, Sable lying over Jocelyn's body.

"As much as I'd like to do this all morning," Jocelyn said, sighing, "I have to go to work today."

Sable shifted her body, and Jocelyn gasped, making Sable grin as she raised her head.

"I suppose if you have to…" Sable said.

"Evil witch…"

"Mm-hmm."

"Come shower with me," Jocelyn said, sitting up and shifting Sable to sit on her lap, leaning in to kiss her again.

Sable smiled. "If you insist."

An hour later, Jocelyn walked into the kitchen dressed in black jeans, black cowboy boots, a slate-gray button-up shirt, and a black belt with a silver buckle. The jacket she wore, black leather with a gray sweatshirt hoodie liner, gave her look its usual butch style.

"Hope you weren't kidding about no suits," she said to Gage, who was standing in the kitchen drinking coffee.

"When have you ever seen me wear a suit?" Gage asked. "You look great."

"Thanks."

"And tired…" Gage said, her look changing to sly.

Jocelyn laughed. "That I am."

"Worth it though?" Gage asked, her smile warm.

"Oh yeah," Jocelyn said, waggling her eyebrows.

Jocelyn loved that Gage never sounded jealous when there was another woman in the picture. Gage was forever rooting for Jocelyn to find "the one." It worried Jocelyn, because she wasn't sure if Gage was even looking for "the one."

"Stop it," Gage said, seeing Jocelyn's look of concern.

"I said nothing."

"I know," Gage said, rolling her eyes. "You don't have to. Just enjoy yourself and be happy. That's all I've ever wanted for you."

Jocelyn nodded. She knew that it was true.

They left for the office a short time later. Jocelyn was driving the Escalade; she planned to start taking her own car soon but wanted to get used to the route first.

"We need to stop and pick up Kit," Gage said.

"You drive your assistant to work…" Jocelyn said with a smirk.

"Shut up, Gun," Gage said automatically, knowing exactly what Jocelyn was thinking.

"So what is the deal there?" Jocelyn asked as she glanced at Gage. "You said her situation is lousy. Is she planning to divorce the guy?"

"I've offered her help if she needs it."

"Of course you have," Jocelyn muttered.

Gage narrowed her eyes. "Shut up, Gun," she said again.

Jocelyn laughed. "Why don't you just rescue her and get it over with?"

"Why don't you just shut up and drive?" Gage said, her smile overly bright.

"Then who would give you shit?"

"Oh, let's see, no one… and that would be just awesome."

"The hell you say," Jocelyn said, glancing over at Gage. "She's jealous, you know."

"Huh?" Gage asked, surprised by the change in topic. "Who?"

"Kit."

"Jealous of who?"

"Me," Jocelyn said. "You didn't see it, huh?"

"I don't know what you're talking about," Gage said. "Kit likes you."

"I didn't say she doesn't like me, Jock. I said she's jealous of me."

"With regard to what?" Gage asked.

"You."

Gage shook her head. "You're crazy. You're always imagining things like that."

"Am I?" Jocelyn asked. "Trust me, babe, you didn't see the wistful looks I saw."

"Wistful?" Gage asked disbelievingly.

"Yeah, especially when you were lying on me that first night," Jocelyn said. "Did you not tell her that we were friends with benefits?"

"I don't remember if I did or not, but she's not into me, Gun. She's busy trying to get her life back."

"And trying to please you," Jocelyn said.

"She works for me. I got her promoted, she's grateful. Jesus, Gun! You're imagining shit."

"Okay," Jocelyn said. "Watch her face when we drive up, when she sees I'm with you."

Gage shook her head. "You are so…"

Sure enough, when they pulled up to the front of Kit's apartment, Kit saw that Jocelyn was driving and her expression changed. Jocelyn looked over at Gage to see if she'd noticed—if she did, Jocelyn couldn't tell—then Kit was climbing into the back seat of the truck.

"Good morning," Gage said, turning her head to greet Kit.

"Hi there," Kit said, smiling.

"Morning," Jocelyn said as she put the truck in gear again.

"Hi," Kit said.

A couple of minutes later, in traffic, Jocelyn stifled a yawn.

"Uh-huh," Gage said, laughing. "This is what happens when you're up half the night acting like a teenager."

"Totally worth the tired."

"And I'm betting it wasn't Sable keeping *you* up, either…" Gage said.

"No, ma'am," Jocelyn said, grinning.

"I'm sorry," Kit said from the back seat. "Did I miss something?"

Sounding a little too hopeful there, girlie, Jocelyn thought. She glanced over at Gage, giving her a "See?" look. Gage just shook her head.

"Jocelyn and Sable were, uh… well… they got together last night."

"Oh, I see," Kit said.

Jocelyn glanced in the rearview mirror and saw Kit's smile.

"I thought your mother brought her home for you," Kit said to Gage.

"Guess I didn't get in there fast enough," Gage said, winking at Jocelyn.

Jocelyn looked openmouthed at Gage. "And I heard you turned her down flat."

"Well, I did tell her I don't date rock stars, that's true."

"So you had your chance," Jocelyn said.

"She's not my type."

"And what is your type, Director McGinnis?" Jocelyn asked pointedly.

"Non rock stars," Gage replied, giving Jocelyn a narrowed look.

Jocelyn shook her head. Her best friend was indeed hopeless.

Jocelyn's first day in the office was somewhat productive. She discovered early on that the people she was in charge of needed very definite guidance. Jocelyn was in charge of the fire and law enforcement side of things, and when she asked one of her new staff for a list of contacts at the various agencies, nothing could be produced.

"You're kidding me, right?" Jocelyn asked.

"No, ma'am," said the man, whose name Jocelyn had already forgotten.

"Okay, well, here's the thing—we need to be able to contact these people in the event of an emergency, and I really don't think that in an emergency we should be scrambling for current contacts," Jocelyn said, doing her best to keep her cool in the face of the stupid man she was dealing with.

"But, ma'am, we can just look it up on the internet." The man was staring at Jocelyn like she was an idiot for not realizing that.

"Does it occur to you that if the emergency is here, we may not have electricity, and that would make it pretty fucking hard to access the internet?" Jocelyn practically growled.

The man looked back at her blankly.

"Just leave," Jocelyn said.

After he left her office, Jocelyn picked up her jacket and walked outside to smoke. She stood against the building. She was just stubbing out her first cigarette when a young blonde came around the corner, almost walking into her.

"Whoa!" Jocelyn said as the girl almost fell backward trying not to run into her. Jocelyn's hand shot out to grab her by the waist.

"Oh my gosh, I'm so sorry!" the girl exclaimed.

"Don't worry about it," Jocelyn said, taking out another cigarette.

"Do you work here?" the girl asked as she took out her own cigarette.

Jocelyn pulled her lighter out and lit the girl's cigarette and her own. "As of today."

"Well, welcome," the girl said. "I'm Kimber."

"Gun," Jocelyn said, extending her hand to the girl.

"Gun?" Kimber repeated.

"Yeah."

"Okay," Kimber said, nodding. "Nice to meet you, Gun."

Jocelyn leaned back against the building again, closing her eyes and turning her face up to the sun that had finally made an appearance that day.

"It's about time we got some family here at OES," Kimber said.

Jocelyn opened one eye. "Family?"

Kimber smiled. "If you're trying to be discreet, you've failed miserably."

Jocelyn chuckled. "Well, you succeeded admirably."

"Thanks, but I'm not trying to hide it. I'm just femme, so no one ever really suspects."

Jocelyn nodded.

"I guess with the new director being gay, they're finally hiring more of us."

"Yeah, I guess so," Jocelyn said. "So what do you think of the new director?"

"Oh my gosh, she is so awesome," Kimber said. "A couple of weeks ago she had this all-hands meeting, and she gave the coolest speech I've ever heard an executive give. She really got everyone motivated, plus…" Kimber grinned. "She's really, really hot."

"Well, she is that, I agree with you there." Jocelyn said. "Well, I better get back inside, before I get into trouble."

"Okay, cool, nice to meet you. Where do you work anyway?"

"Third floor," Jocelyn said as she flipped the girl a wave.

Gage was working in her office when Jocelyn walked in. Gage's phone was plugged in, and the song that was playing was loud and, to Jocelyn's way of thinking, way too heavy rock-wise.

"What in the hell is that?" Jocelyn asked, curling up her lips in disgust, as she gestured to the phone.

"Skrillex, why?" Gage asked.

"It's noise."

Gage stuck her middle finger up at Jocelyn as Kit walked into the office.

"I love seeing the professional interactions of executives," Kit said.

Gage grinned. "Gun always brings it out in me."

"Well, that ought to be fun at meetings," Kit said, chuckling as she did.

"These people need to get a lot less stuffy, a lot faster." Jocelyn shook her head. "By the way, I met a fan of yours outside," she said as she sat down in the chair in front of Gage's desk and put her feet up on the top, crossing them at the ankles.

"Huh?" Gage queried, peering around Jocelyn's cowboy boots.

"I was out smoking, and some kid came out to smoke too. She says you're awesome."

"Well, that's good to know," Gage said. "So did you come to harass me for a reason?"

"I did," Jocelyn said. "How many people can I fire?"

Gage started laughing. "Can you give it more than"—she looked at her watch—"four hours?"

"Not if they're all as dumb as that idiot manager I just talked to," Jocelyn said.

"What's the actual problem?" Gage asked.

"Well, let's see—he doesn't seem to understand the concept that we need up-to-date contacts for all the police and fire departments..."

"Seriously?" Gage asked. "What's his name?"

"Fuck if I know. Something Something Dumbass," Jocelyn said.

Gage laughed, looking over at Kit. "Drew Cummings probably," Kit said.

"Oh," Gage said, nodding. "He's being encouraged to succeed elsewhere, or retire, whichever appeals to him more."

"Yeah, he said we could look the shit up on the internet in the event of an emergency," Jocelyn said.

Gage stared at Jocelyn, stunned, then she smiled. "Remember how much you love me," she said, winking at Jocelyn.

"I'm working on that," Jocelyn said. "Can you work on getting us a helicopter?"

"I'm not sure I have the budget for that," Gage said, used to Jocelyn's quick changes in subject.

"Can you talk to Midnight?" Jocelyn asked. "It would save me having to ask for so many favors from the locals all over the state. I'd rather save our favors for big stuff, you know?"

"Yeah, true. Midnight's not used to having two pilots in charge of this place," Gage said, grinning.

"I won't even charge her pilot's pay," Jocelyn said.

"Can you work up what kind of maintenance budget I'd need to keep one?"

"Of course," Jocelyn said as she stood.

Gage smiled. "Hang in there, Gun. We'll get through this."

"The hell you say," Jocelyn said, winking at Gage.

After Jocelyn left, Gage looked over at Kit. "Can you find me an assistant for her?" she asked. "She really, really hates paperwork. I don't want her to quit before the week is out."

Kit chuckled. "Yeah, I have a couple of ideas."

"Thank you," Gage said, smiling at Kit.

"So her and Sable, huh?" Kit asked, leaning against Gage's desk.

"Yeah," Gage said. "The funny thing is that on Friday she didn't even like her."

"Fine line between love and hate."

"I guess so," Gage said. "So how are things with you?"

"Okay," Kit said. "He's been a little better."

"Good," Gage said. "You remember your promise to me though, right?"

"Did I actually promise?" Kit asked with a smile.

"Don't make me fire you."

"Again?" Kit asked as she handed Gage papers to sign.

"Yep," Gage said, grinning.

Chapter 7

By Thursday a trip to the gym was absolutely necessary. As Gage drove, she noted that Jocelyn was texting. She glanced over pointedly.

"Knock it off," Jocelyn said, grinning.

"Just checking to see if we're texting with our girlfriend like all the kids are doing these days."

"Don't make me smack you," Jocelyn said. "And yes, I'm texting Sable. So what?"

"Are you two going steady?"

"You do remember that I know where you sleep, right?" Jocelyn said, her tone low.

Gage laughed.

"Stop picking on her," Kit said from the back seat. "I think it's really cute."

"Hey, you're supposed to be on my side!" Gage said, glancing at Kit in the rearview mirror.

Jocelyn threw Kit a dirty look. "I don't think I like being referred to as cute."

"See?" Kit said, grinning at Gage.

"Oh, I like it," Gage said.

"I know where you both work…" Jocelyn warned.

"Uh-huh," Gage said, as she pulled into the parking lot of Natalia and Jazmine's studio.

"You going to do the dance class again?" Kit asked.

"Yeah," Gage said. "Kai had been threatening to train me and, frankly, I'm not sure I can handle her level of training just yet. I'm working up to it."

"I wouldn't last ten seconds with Kai," Kit said.

"I may have to give it a shot," Jocelyn said.

"Just to prove again that you're a badass?" Gage asked.

"Yeah, that's it."

During the class, Jocelyn stood with Kit, watching; she'd already talked to Kai about some training and arranged an appointment for the following week. She was waiting for Sable, who was driving the Viper to the studio to pick her up.

"I gotta admit, she looks pretty good doing that," Jocelyn said.

Kit just nodded.

The routine the class was doing required a lot of arm movement. They both saw Gage wince.

"She's hurting her shoulder," Kit said.

"Yep," Jocelyn said. "Jock!" she yelled.

Gage's head snapped around. Jocelyn shook her head, touching her hand to her shoulder. Gage nodded, then continued with the routine, using her arm less.

There was a stir when Sable Sands along with Lenna McGinnis walked into the studio.

Sable walked over to Jocelyn; Jocelyn slid her arm around Sable's shoulder and leaned down to kiss her.

On the floor, Gage saw Cat, who was in front of her, look over at the two that had just entered. She also saw Cat watch as Jocelyn kissed Sable, and saw a flicker of surprise on Cat's face. During the next break, Cat turned to Gage.

"Is Gun with Sable now?" she asked.

"Looks like," Gage said, her smile mild.

Cat nodded. "And Sable thought Gun didn't like her."

"Guess Gun changed her mind."

"I guess so," Cat said, smiling.

On the other side of the half wall, Sable's eyes found Catalina. She felt Jocelyn's arm tighten around her shoulder slightly and glanced up at her.

"Don't let her bother you," Jocelyn told her.

Sable shook her head. "She's not."

Jocelyn nodded, smiling.

The next routine started. Once again, it called for a lot of arm movements, and Gage once again continually did them, wincing as she did.

"She's hurting," Lenna commented from behind Kit and Jocelyn.

"Yep," Jocelyn said.

"You still know how to fix it though, right?" Lenna asked.

"Yeah, but we're going out," Jocelyn said, nodding down at Sable. "Kit knows how to handle our girl. She'll take care of her."

Kit glanced over at Jocelyn, surprised by the way she'd phrased it. Jocelyn simply winked at her, smiling.

"By the way, what are you doing here?" Jocelyn asked Lenna.

"I have a date," Lenna said. "And she's picking me up here. Everyone seems to know this place."

They watched as Gage continued to do the class. When once again she was pushing it and hurting herself, Kit yelled "Director!" to get her to pay attention to her movement.

Kit caught Gage's quick grin and saw that she started taking it easier again.

When the class finally ended, Kit looked at Jocelyn. "She's still moving it, so it's not dislocated, right? 'Cause I don't know how to fix that..."

"Google it," Jocelyn said.

"I did, but I need to see it done in person before I'm going to be brave enough to do it," Kit said.

Jocelyn smiled. The kid was so into Gage it wasn't even funny. The bois had come out to admire Jocelyn's Viper, so Jocelyn was able to check on Gage as she walked to the Escalade.

"You're okay, yeah?" Jocelyn asked.

"I'm fine, Gun, breathe," Gage said. "Go keep the bois from drooling all over your car and ruining your paint job." She winked at her best friend.

After Gage hugged her mom and told her to have a good time on her date, Gage and Kit got into the Escalade. As Gage drove out of the parking lot, Kit could see that she was moving gingerly.

"You're really hurting, aren't you?" Kit asked.

"It's not too bad," Gage said, but as she went to turn the next corner, she winced.

"Yeah, I believe that, totally," Kit said, running her hand over the back of Gage's shoulder. "Oh God, Gage, there's a huge knot."

"It's okay," Gage said.

"We should have stayed in the parking lot. I could have at least done something to try to ease this knot," Kit said.

"Well, you could go home with me and lie on me to do it like Gun does, but I'm betting hubby might have an issue with that." Gage winked at Kit.

Kit shuddered slightly at the thought of lying on Gage "like Gun does" but managed to keep a straight face.

"Well, you need this knot out," she said.

"I'll down some Motrin when I get home and take a hot shower. I should be fine."

Twenty minutes later when Gage went to drop Kit off, Kit insisted on trying to work on the knot in Gage's shoulder. Gage had gotten to the point where she was driving with one hand so as not to move her shoulder. She actually welcomed the massaging that Kit did on it. Fifteen minutes later, Kit got out of the truck. Gage waited until she was safely inside then left. She went home, took Motrin and climbed into a hot shower, staying in it until the water started getting cold. She got out of the shower and dried off, then put on sweat pants and a tank top and went into the kitchen and grabbed a beer.

She had just lain down on her bed when her phone rang. She picked it up.

"Hey, Kit, what's up?"

"Gage…" Kit said, her voice shaking.

Gage sat up immediately. "Kit, what is it? Tell me what's going on," she said, her voice calm as she got up and, putting the phone on speaker, pulled off her sweats and pulled on the jeans she'd discarded earlier. "Kit, honey, talk to me," Gage said louder when Kit didn't say anything else.

"It's Jack… he's… Oh God… Gage…" Kit said, her breath coming in short terrified gasps.

Gage sat down on the bed, pulling on her combat boots.

"Where are you, Kit?" Gage tied her boots as quickly as she could, thanking God for so many drills in the Army that she could do it in her sleep.

"The apartment, in the bathroom," Kit said. Gage could hear pounding on the door and yelling.

"Okay, I'm coming right now," Gage said, putting her holstered gun to the small of her back. "Stay in the bathroom if you can. Find something to use as a weapon, even if you have to break a mirror to do it."

"Okay," Kit said, sounding terrified by the idea.

"Protect yourself, Kit, you hear me?" Gage said, running out to the Escalade and getting in. She started it with a roar. "I'm coming as fast as I can, babe, just hold on. Stay on the phone with me as long as you can, okay?"

"Okay," Kit said, crying now.

"Calm down, honey. Do you have something you can use?" Gage asked.

"I… I don't… I don't know."

"Kit, put the phone down long enough to find something, please, honey," Gage said as she drove down the curved roads near the house as fast as she safely could.

Gage heard breaking glass, and then Kit picked up the phone again.

"Okay," Kit said, her voice tremulous. "Gage, I don't know if I can use this… I don't know if I can…"

"Kit, if it's you or him, babe, I want you to use it, okay? You have the right to defend yourself. Do you understand me?"

"Y-yes…" Kit said, still sounding scared.

"Is Caitlyn there, Kit?" Gage asked.

"No, she's at my mother's house."

Gage breathed a sigh of relief as she got down to North Bronson to get on the freeway. Fortunately, it was getting later in the evening, so traffic was easing.

"Okay. I'm coming, babe, I promise… I'm coming. Just stay calm," Gage said. "Can you tell me what happened that set him off?"

Kit started crying then. "He's... he... I couldn't... he wouldn't let me explain... he thinks... Oh God, Gage, he's so mad. He's going to kill me..."

"No, he's not," Gage told her. "I'm going to get there, and I'm going to deal with him. You just need to stay away from him till I get there, okay?"

"I can hear him throwing things in the other room."

"Better there than where you are, babe," Gage said. "Did you call the police?"

"No!" Kit said. "I can't, Gage... if he goes to jail..." Kit began, her tone climbing hysterically.

"Okay, okay, calm down. We'll deal with it when I get there."

"You're coming now?" Kit's voice was so small and scared that Gage had to swallow against the terror that kept trying to rise in her throat.

She knew that there was very little standing between Jack and Kit. One good kick to the door to the bathroom and he was going to be on her. Gage had no idea if Kit would be brave enough to stab him with whatever glass piece she was holding. It was no easy thing, stabbing another person, and someone as young and innocent as Kit would have a much harder time.

"Yes, honey, I'm on the freeway right now. I'll be there in a few minutes. You just need to hold on, okay?" Gage said, keeping her voice as calm as she possibly could.

She weaved in and out of traffic, even using the emergency lane. She figured if nothing else maybe a cop would get on her tail and follow her to Kit's apartment.

Suddenly there was a loud crash, and Gage knew Jack had just kicked in the door.

"Fuck!" Gage yelled as Kit screamed and the phone went dead with a loud clatter.

She jammed her foot down on the gas pedal, all thoughts of caution gone.

Ten minutes later she was running up the stairs to Kit's apartment. She quickly tried the door; naturally it was locked. Stepping back, she used a well-placed kick to splinter the doorjamb. The door swung open as Gage drew her weapon, and she moved into the apartment, her eyes scanning the area. She heard Kit scream and ran to the side of the open bedroom door.

"Kit!" Gage shouted, her back against the wall on the outside of the bedroom.

"Gage, he has a knife!" Kit yelled.

Gage stepped into the doorway. "Good thing I brought a gun then," she said as she located Jack, holding Kit, a knife to her throat. She trained the weapon on him. "Drop it, Jack, or I swear to God I'll drop you."

"I'll fucking kill her!" Jack yelled.

"Not gonna happen," Gage said, shaking her head.

Gage spared a look at Kit and could see the sheer terror in her eyes.

"Put the knife down now," Gage said, her words slow and measured. Her finger settled on the trigger of her weapon as she lowered her head to line Jack's head up in her sights.

She would be going for the kill shot; she wouldn't take the chance that wounding him would allow him to kill Kit.

"I'm a damned good shot, Jack," Gage said, her voice oozing confidence. "I really don't think you want to test me."

"Fucking dyke!" Jack screamed.

"That being said…" Gage said, smirking, "put the knife down, now, or I'll drop you where you stand."

"You're not a fucking cop!"

"I don't have to be," Gage said, her tone all cop at that moment. "I'm the one holding the gun, and you're holding my friend with a knife to her throat. Threat established and eliminated,"

Kit heard the confidence in Gage's voice, and she could feel Jack trembling. She knew that Gage was scaring him, and she believed that Gage could do exactly what she was saying she could. A sense of calm washed over her. Gage was here now and she was going to save her. Gage wouldn't let Jack hurt her anymore; Kit believed that to her very core.

Jack felt Kit go completely still and actually felt her relax in his grasp. That scared him even more. It was bad enough this dyke bitch was pointing a gun at him, but his wife had that much confidence in the bitch's aim that she wasn't even scared? Fuck this! Jack tossed the knife away and let Kit go.

"Kit, come here," Gage beckoned, wanting Kit as far away from Jack as possible.

Gage holstered her weapon and moved Kit toward the door. She was shocked when she suddenly heard Jack running at her. He grabbed her ponytail. She shoved Kit away from her and spun, throwing a punch that knocked Jack completely out. Unfortunately it also dislocated her shoulder, but she didn't take the time to worry about that. Kit was crying and getting hysterical, so Gage ushered her out of the apartment, down the stairs and into the Escalade.

In the vehicle, Gage turned to Kit. "Are you hurt?"

Kit shook her head, but Gage could see a bruise on her cheek.

"Can we go, please?" Kit asked, her voice bordering on frantic.

"Okay," Gage said.

She knew she needed to report Jack to the cops, but she also knew that Kit was terrified. She started the Escalade using her left hand, since her right hand was tingling and her shoulder was screaming at her. Kit was too out of it to notice.

Gage drove them back to her mother's house and ushered Kit inside. Kit was shaking horribly by then, so Gage walked into the kitchen and poured Kit a shot of tequila.

"Drink it. It'll calm you down," Gage told Kit.

Kit drank the shot, wincing as the alcohol burned down her throat. She did then feel calmer, however. Gage took her into the living room, sat her down and kneeled in front of her, looking her face over. She reached up with her left hand, touching Kit's face next to the darkening bruise on her cheek.

"Is this the only thing?" Gage asked gently.

Kit drew in a sharp breath and nodded, tears in her eyes again.

Gage hugged Kit to her with her left arm, sitting down on the couch next to her. Kit leaned heavily against Gage, crying in earnest now.

"Okay, honey... okay... You're okay now..." Gage said soothingly.

After a long while, it was apparent that Kit was exhausted. Gage stood, taking Kit's hand.

"Come on." She led Kit to one of the guest bedrooms, but Kit shook her head. "Can I stay with you?" she asked, her voice soft.

"Of course," Gage said.

She walked down the hall to the suite of rooms she was using, leading Kit with her. There she sat Kit down on the bed; Kit lay down straight away. Gage removed her holstered weapon from the small of her back and set it on the dresser. She sat down on the bed, unlacing her boots with her left hand and kicking them off.

When she lay back on the bed, Kit immediately moved closer. Fortunately, Kit was on her left side, so Gage was able to put her arm around the girl without pain. When she felt Kit's breath become even, and she was sure the girl was asleep, Gage carefully pulled her phone out of her jeans pocket. She tapped out a message to Jocelyn, asking her to come up to her room when she and Sable got back. Jocelyn replied almost instantly.

Jocelyn: Why what's going on?

Gage could almost feel the tension in Jocelyn's text.

Gage: Shoulder hurt, need relocating.

Jocelyn: Fuckin' A what did you do?

Gage: Knight in shining armor shit.

Jocelyn: Great... Be home soon.

Gage: No rush.

Jocelyn: Sure, right.

Jocelyn looked at Sable. They were just getting the check from the waitress.

"Gotta go home, babe, sorry," Jocelyn said.

"Why? What's going on?" Sable asked, looking worried.

"Gage managed to dislocate her shoulder, somehow. She won't go to a hospital to fix it, so I need to."

Sable stood. "Okay, let's go."

Jocelyn smiled, glad that Sable wasn't upset about cutting their evening short.

In the Viper on the way back to the house, Sable looked over at Jocelyn. "Do you know what she did to dislocate it?"

"The only explanation I got was 'knight in shining armor shit,'" Jocelyn said.

Sable laughed. "And that's an answer you understand, I take it?"

"My bet is she's finally rescued that cute little assistant of hers," Jocelyn said, smiling.

"And that's a good thing?"

"Oh yeah," Jocelyn said. "Gage hasn't really dated anyone for about six years now, so… this is a definite good thing."

"Six years?" Sable said. "Seriously?"

"She hides out with work and with Mark," Jocelyn said. "It's just easier for her."

"Easier?"

"She likes her life compartmentalized. And she likes things simple, not messy. Relationships are messy."

Sable nodded. "Which is why she relies on sex with you when she needs it, right? Because it's simple and she gets what she needs."

Jocelyn glanced at Sable, looking for signs of jealousy. She didn't see any.

"Basically, but don't forget, I used her for the same thing. It wasn't just one sided."

"I know," Sable said. "But it sounds like you dated in between those times."

"Yeah," Jocelyn said. "And she always respected that."

Sable nodded, wondering how long it would be until Gage needed something from Jocelyn again, and if she was going to be able to handle that. She'd had to share Catalina with Elizabeth Endicott, and it hadn't worked in the end. She was thinking she was simply repeating history at this point. Would she ever learn?

At the house, Jocelyn walked upstairs and into the room Gage was using. Sable followed, watching from the doorway. Jocelyn saw Gage lying on the bed, with Kit curled up next to her. Gage's right hand was on her stomach, and Jocelyn could see she was in pain.

"What happened?" Jocelyn whispered as she walked over to the bed.

"I'll tell ya later," Gage whispered back.

"I hope he looks worse."

"He was out cold when I left." Gage's green eyes glittered with remembered malice.

"That's my girl," Jocelyn said, grinning. "Okay, are you seriously going to try to do this while she's asleep next to you?"

"Yeah, it'll be fine."

"Okay."

Gage put her arm down, then slowly moved it to a perpendicular position, at a forty-five-degree angle from her body. Jocelyn clasped her hand in Gage's and kicked off her boots, putting a foot up to Gage's side.

"You ready?" Jocelyn asked. Seeing how much pain Gage was already in, she knew this was going to hurt.

Gage exhaled slowly, then nodded.

Jocelyn gently pulled on Gage's hand, moving her arm in an upward sweeping motion. Gage gritted her teeth and squeezed Jocelyn's hand sharply, then Jocelyn felt the joint pop back into place. Gage let her breath out in a rush, nodding her head.

"Okay, now Vicodin?" Jocelyn asked.

"Yeah, there on the nightstand," Gage said, glancing in that direction.

"Got it." Jocelyn picked up the bottle and took one out for Gage.

Gage opened her mouth, and Jocelyn put it inside. Gage swallowed it.

"Okay, I'm gonna got get you an ice pack," Jocelyn said.

"Thanks," Gage said, smiling tiredly.

Jocelyn came back a minute later and put the ice pack around Gage's shoulder.

"Okay, now go take care of your girl," Gage told Jocelyn with a wink.

"I was," Jocelyn said pointedly. "Now I'll go take care of Sable."

Jocelyn left the room then, seeing that Sable was still standing in the doorway. She took Sable's hand and led her back down to the room she was staying in. Jocelyn took the time to make love to her for hours that night to make up for their lost evening. Sable had to keep pushing away the words "Go take care of your girl" and Jocelyn's response of "I was." It hurt more than Sable wanted to admit.

It had Sable telling Jocelyn the next day that she was headed back to London after the weekend.

"Okay," Jocelyn said, looking surprised. "When will you be back?"

"Well, I live in London," Sable said offhandedly.

Jocelyn's expression was a mixture of surprise and wariness. Finally she nodded, getting out of bed and going to take a shower. She had planned to take the day off that day but decided going to work was now a good way to deal with this news.

Sable lay in bed, staring up at the ceiling. She knew that she'd pissed Jocelyn off, but she wasn't about to play second fiddle; she just couldn't do it again. It was better this way, end it cleanly. She just hadn't thought it would hurt so much to do it.

***

Kit woke up early the next morning; it took her a moment to realize where she was. Before she even opened her eyes she could smell

Gage's cologne close to her. She breathed it in, and then opened her eyes. Gage's arm was around her, and Gage was asleep on her back.

Kit thought back over the night before. She'd gone up to the apartment after getting out of the Escalade. Jack had been home and had told her that her mother had Caitlyn at her house. She'd made dinner, and they'd eaten. Afterwards, while she was clearing the table, he'd grabbed her, his face lustful. She'd pushed him away, which had only made him pull her closer.

"I can fucking smell her on you!" he growled. "Are you fucking that dyke?" It wasn't the first time he'd asked it, but Kit realized that she probably smelled like Gage because she'd been massaging her shoulder, which had put her close.

"No, stop it, Jack," Kit had said, pulling away from him again.

He'd grabbed her then, and when she tried to get away he'd hit her. There'd been a struggle, and she'd finally made it to the bathroom, locking the door. In her terrified state it had taken her a while to decide to call Gage.

She thought about how Gage had talked to her the entire time as she was coming to save her. She'd called her "honey" and "babe," and it had calmed her. When Jack had kicked in the bathroom door she'd been terrified. She'd tried to do what Gage had told her, but Jack had easily overpowered her and knocked the glass from her hand. She'd run out of the bathroom and tried to get to the door, but he'd caught up to her and grabbed her again.

He'd had her on the bed and was intent on raping her when there'd been a huge crash at the front of the apartment. Kit had screamed, praying it was Gage. Jack had dragged her off the bed and put the knife to her throat, telling her he'd slit her throat before that "dyke cunt" would have her. When Gage had screamed her name, Kit had known she needed to tell Gage that Jack had a knife. She was more worried about Jack hurting Gage at that point. When Gage had stepped into the doorway, her gun drawn, it had been the most wonderful thing Kit had ever seen.

Kit thought about what Gage had said to Jack, telling him she'd kill him before he could hurt Kit. When Jack had finally tossed the knife aside, Kit had run to Gage. Gage had been ushering her toward the door when... then Kit remembered that Jack had grabbed Gage, and Gage had... she'd hit him, with her right arm.

"Oh God," Kit said, sitting up and looking down at Gage's right shoulder in the dim morning light.

Her movement woke Gage. "What's wrong?"

"You hit him... you hit him with your right hand..." Kit said.

"Because I'm right handed."

"But your shoulder!"

"Was dislocated and isn't anymore, thanks to Gun." Gage sat up, touching her left hand to Kit's face. "I'm okay. The question is how are you?"

"No," Kit said, "that isn't the question. You are still using your left hand, which means your right shoulder still hurts."

Gage grinned. "Well, Vicodin wears off eventually."

Kit put her hand to Gage's shoulder. Sliding her hand around, she immediately felt the vicious knot at the back. Kit moved to get on Gage's right side, putting her body against Gage's to use her body heat to warm the muscles.

"It's probably going to be easier if you lie back down," Kit said.

Gage chuckled as she did what she was told. Kit began to rub the knot in Gage's shoulder. It took a while, but the muscle finally started to loosen up. When the knot was no longer there, Kit curled the upper part of her body against Gage's shoulder, to keep the muscle warm so it would have a chance to fully relax.

Gage reached back and touched Kit's thigh, which was pressed against her rear due to Kit having shifted up behind Gage. Kit put her hand to the front of Gage's right shoulder, the side of her face against Gage's head. They lay that way for a while, both of them closing their eyes.

After a half an hour, Gage turned her head up toward Kit. At the same time, Kit lifted her head and gazed down at this woman that was her boss—the woman who had literally saved her life the night before. Kit's breath caught in her throat as Gage's right hand touched the back of Kit's head, pulling her down to kiss her. Gage's lips were gentle at first. Kit's soft moan as her body lit up with sensations had Gage deepening the kiss as she shifted to lie on her back. Gage moved her right arm under Kit to pull her over her body, their lips never parting.

Kit grasped at Gage's left shoulder and shirt as Gage touched her face, continuing to kiss her, her mouth becoming more insistent. Kit shifted her body to lie over Gage, pressing closer. Gage slid her right leg between Kit's legs and brought her right hand down to Kit's hips, pressing her closer still and moving to cause friction. Within minutes Kit was moaning and gasping. Gage moved her lips to Kit's neck, then to her ear.

"Come with me, honey…" Gage said, her voice husky, her breathing heavy too.

That sent Kit over the edge, and she came with an outcry. Gage came with her, pressing Kit down harder on her as she did.

Afterwards, Kit lay against Gage, her forehead on Gage's left shoulder, breathing heavily. Gage stroked Kit's back as she did her best to calm her pulse as well.

"I've wanted that for a long time now," Kit said softly.

Gage glanced up at her. "You have?"

Kit nodded.

"Jos thought you were jealous of her," Gage said, her tone questioning even though she didn't ask an actual question.

"I was," Kit said.

"Why?"

"Because she knew you, she had you… has you," Kit said, trying to make sense.

"Jos and I are friends, Kit, that's all," Gage said.

"But you sleep with her," Kit said, shaking her head. "I wanted that with you."

"Well, I'd say you just got it," Gage said, grinning. "No matter how much fucking trouble I'm going to get into for sleeping with someone who works for me."

Kit bit her lip. "I hadn't really thought about that."

"I just didn't care at that point," Gage said, smiling lasciviously.

"Mmm…" Kit murmured.

They lay quietly for a while, then Gage shifted Kit to her left side.

"Later this morning we're going to your mother's to get Caitlyn, and I'm calling the local PD to pick up Jack."

Kit's eyes widened. "But—"

"No buts, Kit. He would have killed you last night, and if Caitlyn had been there he would have killed her too."

Kit's lips trembled upon hearing that.

"He needs to go to jail," Gage said.

Kit started to shake her head. "You don't understand, Gage. I can't—"

"You and Caitlyn will stay here with me until I get a place of my own, and then you can come stay there with me."

"I can't do that," Kit said. "This isn't your responsibility."

Gage sighed. "Let's just take this one step at a time, okay?"

"Okay." Kit looked worried, but she didn't say any more about the future.

Later that morning Gage contacted Commerce Police Department. She reported the incident at the apartment the night before. She explained who she was, and that she had a concealed carry weapons permit and that her employee had been in danger. She detailed the incident and told them she'd be down to make an official statement. They told her that they'd make contact with Jack and arrest him for spousal abuse. They asked that Kit make a statement as well. It took some convincing, but Kit agreed to swear out a statement about the incident.

They also went to Kit's mother's house and picked up Caitlyn. While Gage entertained Caitlyn, Kit told her mother what had happened. Kit explained to her mother that she and Caitlyn would be staying with Gage. Tina was happy to hear it; she liked Gage and knew that Kit would be safe with her. Tina was fully aware of her daughter's sexual preference and hadn't been happy when Kit had saddled herself with Jack.

When they left, Tina hugged Gage, thanking her for rescuing Kit.

Kit, Gage and Caitlyn went back to Gage's house. Kit and Gage had stopped by the apartment before going to Kit's mom's house, to pick up clothes and items that Kit and Caitlyn would need for a while.

That night, Kit and Caitlyn went to sleep in one of the guest bedrooms. Kit and Gage hadn't wanted to freak Caitlyn out with their changed relationship. Even so, Gage had hugged Kit when she'd walked them to the guest room, kissing her softly on the cheek.

Gage was lying on her bed on her left side. She'd just dozed off when she felt the lightest touch on her arm near her shoulder. She opened her eyes and saw that Caitlyn was sitting on the bed next to where she lay.

"Hi," Gage said, smiling at the girl.

Caitlyn smiled softly.

"Are you lost?" Gage asked.

Caitlyn shook her head, her blue eyes like Kit's wide. She reached out and touched Gage's tattoo, running her finger down it and then looking at her finger.

Gage smiled. "It doesn't come off, honey."

Caitlyn stared at her like she had to be joking.

Gage licked her own finger and rubbed it down the tattoo, then showed her finger to Caitlyn. "See?"

Caitlyn blinked a couple of times, then nodded.

"So do you want me to take you back to your mom?" Gage asked softly.

Caitlyn shook her head vehemently.

"Okay... can you tell me what you want?" Gage asked then.

Caitlyn simply blinked again, then screwed her lips up.

"Caitlyn, are you scared?" Gage asked, sensing the tension in the girl.

Caitlyn nodded.

"Is it the house?" Gage asked. "It's really big, I know."

Caitlyn shook her head.

"Then what are you afraid of, honey? You can tell me."

Caitlyn looked scared.

"Do you trust me?" Gage asked softly.

Caitlyn nodded again.

"Then tell me what you're afraid of."

"Him," Caitlyn said softly.

Gage drew her breath in. "He's never going to hurt you or your mommy again, I promise you that. Okay?"

Caitlyn nodded, seeming relieved. She lay down next to Gage. Gage smiled, remembering when Mark would do the same thing after his dad was killed.

"Let's at least text your mom to let her know where you are, so she doesn't worry, okay?" Gage asked.

Again, Caitlyn nodded.

Gage picked up her phone and tapped out a message to Kit, telling her that Caitlyn was with her in her room if she was looking for her. She showed the phone to Caitlyn.

"See that button right there?" Gage said, pointing. "That says 'send.' Can you hit that for me?"

Excitedly, Caitlyn reached out one little finger to touch the button. Gage had turned the sound up on the phone so Caitlyn could hear the whooshing sound when the message was sent.

"Hear that?" Gage said, putting her ear near her phone. "The message elves just ran off with the message to take it to your mom. Let's just hope they're quiet so they don't wake her up."

Caitlyn smiled. "Elves?"

"Yeah," Gage said, holding her thumb and forefinger a quarter inch apart. "Little tiny ones."

Caitlyn giggled and lay down, putting her head on Gage's shoulder and reaching up to trace the tattoo there. It was the first thing Kit saw when she walked into the room. She stood back, watching Gage interact with her daughter.

Gage had turned her arm so Caitlyn could easily reach her tattoo.

"What this?" Caitlyn asked.

"It's called a Celtic cross," Gage said. "It's Irish, like me."

"Irish?" Caitlyn queried.

"My ancestors are from Ireland," Gage said. "It's an island."

"Can I be Irish?"

"Sure. Your name, Caitlyn, is actually an Irish name," Gage said, smiling. "But you might be something even cooler than Irish. Maybe you want to be that too."

"No, Irish," Caitlyn said petulantly.

"Okay, Irish you are." Gage smiled, then she caught sight of Kit standing in the doorway. "Uh-oh, the elves woke up Mommy."

"Elves?" Kit asked as she walked into the room.

"In the phone, Mommy." Caitlyn pointed to Gage's phone lying on the nightstand. "Didn't they bring you the message?"

"Well, of course they did," Kit said, sitting next to where Caitlyn lay next to Gage.

"And they waked you up?"

"Yes, they *woke* me up," Kit said, glancing at Gage. "I'm so sorry, Gage."

"She's fine," Gage said.

Kit shook her head. "But you have a hard enough time sleeping…"

"I wasn't asleep."

"And you'll never get to sleep with chatterbox here," Kit said.

"Tell you what," Gage said, looking at Caitlyn and then at Kit. "Why don't we all just sleep right here?"

"Gage…" Kit began.

"Sleep here, Mommy!" Caitlyn exclaimed.

Kit looked at Gage, and Gage smiled softly, nodding her head.

"Okay, let's try it," Kit said. "But, Caitlyn Marie, you will sleep or we go back in the other room. Director McGinnis needs to get her rest."

"Director?"

"It means she's the big boss."

Caitlyn gazed up at Gage, her eyes wide. Gage winked at Caitlyn.

The three settled down, Kit on one side of Caitlyn and Gage on the other. Caitlyn lay on her back, putting her hands out to both Kit and Gage and taking their hands. Gage put her arm up over Caitlyn's head and reached down to touch Kit's hair, stroking it gently. Their eyes met over Caitlyn, and they both smiled. Caitlyn was asleep a few minutes later.

"Thank you for being so good with her," Kit said to Gage.

"I did raise a son, remember?" Gage said, smiling.

"I know, but he was yours. This is different."

"She's a child, Kit. It doesn't matter to me that she's not mine," Gage said. "You know, she told me she's afraid of 'him.'"

Kit felt the comment like a punch to the stomach. She shook her head sadly. "I had hoped I'd shielded her enough from it... I guess not."

"Kids have an amazing way of sensing everything. She may have simply sensed your fear and took it into herself. Regardless, you did the right thing today to get him away from both of you."

"I know," Kit said. "Thank you for that. I don't know if I'd have been brave enough to do it on my own."

"Well, you're not alone, Kit, okay? You have me, you have Jos, you even have the group if you need any of them."

"They'd help me?" Kit asked.

"Yeah," Gage said, smiling. "They're amazing like that, from what I've seen and heard."

Kit nodded, blinking.

"I need to get back together with Memphis. She's been wanting to hang out. I just haven't been able to figure out when yet."

"We'll make a point of it, soon, okay?" Gage said.

Kit smiled. "We, huh?"

"We," Gage said, nodding.

Kit bit her lip. She wasn't sure what Gage meant, but she knew she absolutely needed the woman at that moment. She was also thoroughly enjoying this different level with her. Kit fell asleep with one hand in her daughter's hand, and the other hand clasped in Gage's just above Caitlyn's head.

Gage fell into a sound sleep with a little hand holding hers, and her hand in Kit's, feeling very settled and content suddenly.

***

Things that day at the office became quite unsettled for Jocelyn. She spent most of the day buried deep in maps, boundaries and who served what areas. By three o'clock her brain was aching, and she knew she needed to take a break. Putting on her jacket and sliding her gun into place at her back, legal thanks to a CCW provided by Midnight Chevalier, she walked out of the office.

She made her way out of the front doors to the building and was just lighting a cigarette when Kimber walked out. Kimber smiled at Jocelyn, her eyes surveying the woman. Jocelyn hadn't bothered to dress up at all since it was a Friday. She wore faded jeans, black combat boots, a black tank top and an Army-green zip-up hoodie that said "Army" in white on the side, with an Army patch over the left breast pocket.

"You didn't tell me you were the deputy director," Kimber chastised.

"You didn't ask," Jocelyn said, leaning against a column in the front of the building.

"I asked where you worked."

Jocelyn grinned. "And I told you the third floor."

"The third floor houses more than the deputy director and director's offices," Kimber said.

Jocelyn shrugged, taking a deep draw on her cigarette.

"So where are you headed?" Kimber asked.

"I was headed out to get something to eat."

"Want company?"

Jocelyn narrowed her eyes. "It depends. Are you asking the deputy director, or are you asking Gun?"

"I don't really like executives," Kimber said. "So I'm definitely asking Gun."

"Then yes, I'd love some company," Jocelyn said, smiling.

They walked out to the parking lot. Jocelyn led her over to her Viper.

"This is your car?" Kimber asked, running her hand over the matte Army-green paint.

"Yeah," Jocelyn said as she walked around to open the passenger door for Kimber. "Why?"

"Not very executive-looking," Kimber said, grinning.

"Not trying to be."

A few minutes later they were on the freeway. Jocelyn's hand rested on the center console. Kimber looked over at her.

"So is Gun your nickname? 'Cause that's not the name listed on the org chart."

"Jocelyn Gunnar Mann," she said. "But it's also a nickname, because I was a gunner in the Army."

"A gunner?"

"Yeah, on a helicopter."

"Oh. That's kinda sexy," Kimber said.

Jocelyn raised an eyebrow at the girl but didn't reply.

"So," Kimber said, touching Jocelyn's hand that rested on the center console, her fingers sliding seductively over Jocelyn's, "do you have a girlfriend?"

Jocelyn looked at Kimber sharply, and then thought of what Sable had said that morning: "Well I live in London." Just like that.

Jocelyn shook her head. "No, I don't."

"Do you want one?" Kimber asked, her smile as seductive as her fingers were on Jocelyn's hand.

"No," Jocelyn said.

Kimber licked her lips. "S'okay, I don't have to be your girlfriend to sleep with you."

Jocelyn gave Kimber a surprised look, then her eyes narrowed as she stared pensively at the girl.

Kimber laughed. "Don't worry, this has nothing to do with work," she said. "I don't even need that job. I've just thought you were hot since I met you. The fact that you didn't try to pull out who you really were only made you more appealing to me."

"What do you mean by you don't need the job?" Jocelyn asked.

"My family is rich," Kimber said. "I'm just doing this for the 'job experience,' according to my dad," she said, using air quotes.

"I see," Jocelyn said.

Kimber took Jocelyn's hand, putting it on her leg. She then pushed Jocelyn's hand down to her knee, which was bare because she wore a skirt, and looked at Jocelyn pointedly.

Jocelyn got the hint and slid her hand over Kimber's bare leg, touching the inner part of her knee, then sliding up an inch. Kimber hunched down in the seat slightly, parting her legs. The simple movement sent Jocelyn's hand higher up her bare inner thigh.

"Mmm," Kimber murmured softly. "Should I tell you about some of the fantasies I've had about you since I met you?" she asked, so sexily that Jocelyn felt her body react simply to the tone and the words the girl was saying.

Kimber was what the Army's English counterparts would have called a "comer." She was sexy, young, beautiful, and certainly not afraid to take what she wanted. It was the exact balm Jocelyn's ego needed.

"Is this too freaky for you?" Kimber asked, glancing at Jocelyn.

"I've done much worse," Jocelyn said wryly.

"Ohh..." Kimber murmured excitedly.

Jocelyn slid her hand further up Kimber's leg, and Kimber spread her legs wider, making all kinds of moaning and gasping sounds. When Jocelyn got to the top of Kimber's thighs, while still driving along the freeway, she wasn't completely surprised to find that Kimber wore no panties. Sliding her finger between Kimber's pussy lips, she also found that the girl was incredibly wet.

Jocelyn couldn't stop the hissing sound that escaped her; finding that the girl was that hot and ready to go was beyond erotic. She moved her fingers against Kimber's wetness, and Kimber moaned, grabbing Jocelyn's hand to keep her from removing it. Continuing to move her fingers, Jocelyn could feel Kimber getting hotter and wetter. Before long, Kimber was crying out and rubbing herself against Jocelyn's finger as she came.

When she finally released Jocelyn's wrist, Jocelyn slid her finger over Kimber's wet pussy one more time. Kimber shuddered and gasped again. When Jocelyn removed her hand she pointedly rubbed her thumb and forefinger together. Kimber moaned again.

"Oh my God, that was so fucking hot," Kimber said.

"That wasn't anything," Jocelyn said, grinning.

"Mmm... then take me somewhere and show me what you've got."

"Do you have a place?" Jocelyn asked.

"I do, but don't you?"

Jocelyn chuckled. "Well, I'm staying at Gage's mother's place right now. I just moved here not too long ago, and right now I need to stay away from there, so if you've got a place…"

"Oh yeah, I do," Kimber said. "Take the next exit."

"Your place isn't Daddy's place, is it? 'Cause I really don't need a scene right now."

"No," Kimber said, laughing "It's my place. But I do have a roommate…" Her voice trailed off sexily.

"A roommate?"

"Yeah, and she absolutely loves butches too," Kimber said meaningfully.

"Well… let the games begin, then," Jocelyn said.

She spent the entire weekend with Kimber and her roommate, Donna. It was definitely a good, good weekend. She rarely thought of Sable, and when she did, she just made another round with the girls and the thought was pushed aside.

Chapter 8

"Where the hell have you been?" Gage asked Jocelyn on Monday morning as she walked into Jocelyn's office.

Jocelyn had her head down on her desk. "Don't start on me, Jock. It was a... helluva weekend," she said, smiling roguishly.

"Jesus Christ," Gage muttered. "Haven't you grown out of that kind of thing?"

Jocelyn gave Gage a shocked look. "If I ever get that fucking old, just shoot me, will ya?"

Gage stared back at Jocelyn. "What's going on, Gun? You were God knows where all weekend, and Sable left for London today..."

Jocelyn shook her head. "Don't wanna talk about it."

Gage gave Jocelyn a measured look, knowing that Jocelyn probably should talk about whatever it was, but she also knew that if she pushed, Jocelyn could push back hard. She couldn't afford to get into a huge fight with Jocelyn, so she let it go.

"We need to get to work on some of that disaster-recovery shit for here," Gage said. "The last director didn't even bother. I guess he assumes that natural disasters don't happen here."

Jocelyn reached for her coffee. She knew she needed to get her head back together, even though she was running on around five hours of sleep for the entire weekend.

"So what do you need me to do?" she asked.

"Well, we need to scout an alternate location to man the office in case an airplane falls on this one or something."

"Okay. Tell me what I'm looking for."

"We need something on a separate power grid, it needs to have redundancy systems, and we need to be able to wire up there. We need to be able to transfer operations to it almost instantly. Can you work with Harley and Shen on this?"

"Yeah, you got it," Jocelyn said.

Gage looked at her best friend. "You look like death warmed up, Jos. How much sleep did you get this weekend?"

"Bout five." Jocelyn grinned unrepentantly.

"We aren't kids anymore, Jos—you can't survive on that. Fuck, I don't even want to send you home because I'm worried you'd fall asleep on the drive. Hit the couch in that empty office, get at least four, then we'll talk, okay?"

"Jock, I'm fine—"

Gage shook her head. "Go, now, or I swear I'll have someone drive you home."

"I'm a fuckin' adult," Jocelyn muttered under her breath, even as she got up from her desk.

"Adults remember they have responsibilities, Gun," Gage replied, shooing her out of her own office.

Back in her office, Kit walked in, smiling.

"So where was she?" Kit asked.

"Apparently whoring," Gage said.

Kit grimaced. "Did she say what happened between her and Sable?"

"She didn't want to talk about it."

Kit pressed her lips together in concern. "Can't make her talk?"

"You push Gun, she pushes back, hard," Gage said. "I don't want to get into a nasty fight with her right now, especially not in the office. If she keeps it up, I'll jump her shit at the house."

Kit nodded, looking worried.

"Don't worry. I'll make sure Caitlyn isn't there when I do it."

Kit pressed her lips together. It amazed her that Gage thought of things like that; most people wouldn't. It was Gage's mother's home, after all, and Kit and Caitlyn were just visitors. Not that Lenna McGinnis had treated them like anything but family from the minute she'd met them. Lenna had had a grand time with Caitlyn, telling Gage over and over again that she'd always wished that she and Nick would have had a second child and that it would have been a little girl.

Kit had felt very welcomed by Lenna, and it had gone a long way to make her feel better about staying there. She still wasn't sure what she was going to do long term, but for now, she was perfectly happy with the situation.

Turning around, Kit closed and locked Gage's door. She walked over and put her arms around Gage. Gage smiled down at her.

"What's this about?" Gage asked, her green eyes sparkling.

"I just want to hug you and I don't want anyone walking in on us," Kit said, wrapping her arms around Gage's shoulders. "Thank you… for everything. You are so incredible, I don't know what I would have ever done without you."

Gage pulled Kit closer, then kissed her, deepening the kiss a moment later.

"Director…" Kit murmured, her voice shocked but her grin spoiling the effect.

"Well, hell, if the door is locked," Gage said, grinning too.

Kit giggled, kissing Gage quickly on the lips again. "We have to be professional."

"Yes, ma'am," Gage said, smiling.

Kit walked back over to the door and unlocked it, shaking her head at Gage as she walked back out to her desk.

"Gage, Shiloh's here to see you," Kit called a few minutes later.

"Come on in, Shiloh," Gage called.

Shiloh was Harley Davidson's assistant, and they'd been a package deal. Gage had been told in no uncertain terms by Harley herself that if Shiloh didn't come to OES too, then she wouldn't be making the transition. Harley Davidson was an incredibly talented programmer who could make computers sing, dance, and even tip their hats if she put her mind to it. Gage hadn't hesitated in hiring Shiloh along with Harley.

The beautiful girl that was not only Harley's assistant but her girlfriend as well walked in and sat in the chair in front of Gage's desk. Gage caught sight of Harley walking outside, her headphones in her ears and her head moving to the music. Harley held a lit cigarette and was obviously lost in serious thought.

"Uh… should I be worried that Harley is off on a march?" Gage said. "Did someone upset her?"

Shiloh laughed. "No people upset Harley," she said. "Programs upset Harley."

Gage gave Shiloh a sidelong look. "Would you mind explaining that?"

Shiloh smiled fondly; she was always having to explain her highly eccentric girlfriend to people.

"Harley is heavily ADHD—I'm sure Jericho told you that, right?"

"Yeah," Gage said, "but I don't know much about ADHD either."

"Well, with Harley, it means her mind goes all the time, and her focus is almost always on computer programs, program language, problem solving."

"Okay," Gage said, waiting for the rest.

"Harley is probably one of the most non-confrontational people you'll ever meet, and I know it sounds bad, but it's basically because she really doesn't care what people think of her."

"That's a good thing," Gage said.

"It is, but it also means that she doesn't try to placate people by acting a certain way, or in any way that people might expect."

"So, she does her thing, and if people don't like it, too bad?" Gage asked.

"Pretty much," Shiloh said.

Gage looked at Shiloh, wondering how interesting that was to live with.

"Don't get me wrong," Shiloh said, seeing Gage's look. "Harley is the most loving, loyal and sweet human being on the planet. She deeply cares about people she considers friends, and she will turn herself inside out to do things for them."

"And workwise?"

"Once she's dedicated to a project, she'll kill herself to make it work," Shiloh said. "But that's where I come in."

"Meaning?" Gage asked, trying to understand the dynamic between her new chief information officer and this girl.

"Meaning that Harley will never be in your face about problems in her department, but I will be," Shiloh said with a direct look. "And when I think she's pushing her limits or overdoing it, I'll be letting you know and will be taking her offline until she's back up to full strength."

"Offline…" Gage repeated.

Shiloh chuckled. "I've been hanging out with a programmer pretty much twenty-four-seven for the last two years—I've been infected with her lingo."

"So you're going to be the one that keeps her sane and keeps me up to date," Gage said simply.

"You got it," Shiloh said, her moss-green eyes sparkling. "So let's talk about your audits manager…"

"Uh-oh," Gage said.

"Yeah. She's starting to piss me off, and that's not a good thing… because then Harley suddenly doesn't have time for her projects." She said the last with narrowed eyes.

Gage chuckled. "I'll talk to her."

"Thank you," Shiloh said, smiling.

Meanwhile, Harley walked out of the local convenience store, lighting a cigarette and carrying the Monster Java she'd just bought, her headphones still blaring with music. She didn't look anything like the executive she was. On this particular day she wore dark blue jeans and a faded *Dark Side of the Moon* Pink Floyd T-shirt, with black leather Harley-Davidson boots and a black leather biker jacket. Her long white-blond hair was up in a messy ponytail, her two bright rainbow braids hanging halfway down her chest. She wore four hoops in each ear, and a silver chain with a rainbow feather hanging from the bottom holes. Harley Davidson was a very striking character.

Kimber noticed her right away, in the same way she'd noticed Jocelyn Mann the week before. She was hot and stood out.

"You're the new CIO," Kimber said as Harley walked up to the building, leaning against a column to finish her cigarette.

Harley's blue eyes stayed on her for a long moment, then she nodded, taking another draw on her cigarette.

Kimber smiled. "None of you look like executives, that's for sure."

"I don't think any of us are trying to," Harley said, taking a drink of her Monster Java.

"It's kinda hot," Kimber said.

Harley's gaze flickered. She knew who this girl was, and she knew that she'd been keeping company with Jocelyn.

"If you say so," Harley said, her blue eyes unreadable.

"So is it true that your assistant is also your girlfriend?" Kimber asked.

"Yes, it is."

Kimber made a sucking sound through her teeth as she shook her head regretfully. "That's a shame."

"Why's that?" Harley asked.

"'Cause you're damned hot. All of you are."

"All of us?" Harley asked quizzically.

"All the new executives that the director has brought in. Well, except for the guy. He's hot too; I'm just not into guys," Kimber said, smiling.

Harley nodded. "Okay."

"So are you and your girl exclusive?" Kimber asked.

Harley stared at the girl, wondering if she was going to proposition all of them. She nodded again, perplexed.

"Do you two ever share?" Kimber asked, her smile wicked.

"No," Harley said.

"Well, that's a shame," Kimber said again.

"I'm sure." Harley stubbed out her cigarette. "See ya later."

"Bye," Kimber said, grinning.

Later, Harley was back in her office when a man walked in without knocking. Harley didn't even notice him because she was deep into her work and her music was on loud. "Californication" by the Red

Hot Chili Peppers was playing, and she was singing along to the line about Hollywood selling Californication.

His loud offended gasp was what brought her out of her trance. She glanced at him, reaching over to turn down her music and looking toward her outer office where Shiloh usually sat. Shiloh wasn't at her desk, so Harley turned back to the man who was standing in front of her desk looking very put out.

"Can I help you…" Harley trailed off as she realized she couldn't remember his name.

"Bob, Bob Steephill," he snapped. "I sent you an email. Did you get it?"

Harley widened her blue eyes and blinked a couple of times. "Well, no, but can you tell me what it said?"

Bob shook his head angrily. "What's the point in sending you an email if you don't read it!"

"Sir, I get hundreds of emails a day." Harley's tone was even, but the expression on her face was completely guileless. Bob didn't see that, however.

"Well, Jesus H. Christ!" he exclaimed.

Harley's face reflected her shock and vague alarm at the man's obvious ire. She reached behind her, scratching just above where the gun was nestled at the small of her back. It was an unconscious show of fear and her reaction to that, which was that she'd protect herself in any way she needed to. Her blue eyes continued to stare at the man.

"If you'll just tell me—" Harley began again, in a reasoning tone.

"No! This is ridiculous!" Bob raged.

"Mr. Steephill!" Shiloh barked sharply from Harley's doorway.

Harley could see that Shiloh was fairly enraged. Harley grinned as she turned back to her computer. Bob seemed surprised by Shiloh's outburst and looked at her, and then made the mistake of dismissing her. He turned back to Harley and realized that Harley had basically dismissed him. She was now tapping away at her keyboard again and had turned her music back up. Shiloh, with a very irritated look on her face, put her hand up, gesturing with her index finger for him to come over to her. There was a comical moment when Bob realized that he was about to be taken to task by an assistant.

Shiloh waited for Bob to walk over to her, and she gestured for him to leave Harley's office. He did so in a huff. Shiloh glanced back over at Harley, seeing her head bouncing to her music, as usual; Harley was completely unfazed by another person's ire. Shiloh loved that about her.

Shiloh walked over to where Bob stood stiffly waiting for her.

"First of all, I'm sure you know better than to talk to any executive that way, but let me tell you something," Shiloh said, leaning on the edge of her desk and looking far from intimidated. "If you ever talk to *my* executive like that again, I'll make sure Director McGinnis hears about it. Are we clear?" Shiloh had emphasized the word "my" because she wanted to make sure he understood that she would protect Harley no matter what.

The rumor about Shiloh being Harley's girlfriend had already circulated, and Shiloh didn't give one damn about that. What she gave a damn about was people not understanding that she would not put up with anyone taking advantage of Harley. Harley Marie Davidson was a very pure spirit, and she was not the kind of person to push back when someone pushed at her. Shiloh, however, in falling in love with everything that Harley was, had developed a serious protective streak when it came to her girlfriend. More than one person at the Department of Justice had been on the receiving end of Shiloh's wrath when they'd mistreated Harley. It looked like that was going to continue at OES.

"Now, if you have any kind of complaint, it should be sent to me, as I explained to every manager in our very first meeting. Harley does not deal with day-to-day details or with people. I deal with people, and I don't deal well with people that get nasty with Harley," Shiloh told the man sharply. "If you want to explain the problem to me, I would be happy to see what we can do."

Bob stared at Shiloh, stunned by her statements and unable to formulate an intelligent reply.

"This is highly irregular!" he finally exclaimed.

"I understand that," Shiloh said, not looking the least bit apologetic about that fact. "But it is how Harley and I do things, so you might want to get used to it."

After Shiloh finished dealing with Bob, she walked into Harley's office and stood behind her, putting her hands on Harley's shoulders and kissing her on the temple.

"You okay?" Harley asked as she came out of her programmer's trance once again.

Shiloh leaned against the counter next to where Harley sat. Harley had insisted on modular furniture in her office, hating the "executive look" for furniture; it wasn't proper computer furniture to Harley.

"I'm fine," Shiloh said. "I just hate that we have to now teach a whole new set of people how not to act around you."

Harley smiled. "You know I don't really care about that, right?"

"I know," Shiloh said, handing her a sandwich. "I step out to grab you some lunch and someone attempts to accost you."

"He was just being irate," Harley said. "I'm armed."

"I know, I saw that little gesture," Shiloh said, reaching to her back and scratching like Harley had.

"Oh, did I do that?" Harley asked, grimacing slightly.

"You did," Shiloh said. "Eat, babe." She gestured to the sandwich she'd just handed her.

Harley nodded, her eyes already moving back to the computer screen, unconsciously setting the sandwich back down as her fingers itched to get back on the keyboard.

"Don't make me turn it off..." Shiloh threatened, picking up the sandwich and handing it to Harley.

Harley laughed, leaning back in her chair, and putting a booted foot up on the counter next to Shiloh's hip. "That sounds like a threat."

"It was," Shiloh said, glancing up as she saw a young woman who had a very definite soft-butch vibe to her standing in the doorway to Harley's office. "Can I help you?"

"Uh, yeah," the young woman stammered, her eyes going from Shiloh to Harley, then back to Shiloh. "I have an issue. I was told the deputy director had an open-door policy..."

Shiloh looked down at Harley. "You eat," she told Harley, then she smiled at the young woman. "Come on in."

The woman walked in, taking off her backward-facing ball cap and running her hand through her short dark hair. She sat in the chair across from Harley. Her eyes took in the posters that Harley had hanging in her office, seeing one that said "Programmers are tools for converting caffeine to code."

"That one's awesome," she said, pointing at the poster and smiling widely.

In that moment, Shiloh knew it was safe to leave this young woman alone with Harley. She was obviously a programmer like Harley; Shiloh knew they'd speak the same language. She moved from where she was leaning, giving Harley a firm look.

"I get that you're about to get completely entrenched in programmer-speak, but you eat that sandwich or I'm coming back in here and removing your keyboard," Shiloh said, winking at the young woman as she did.

"That's cold," the young woman said, grinning.

Harley grinned back. "She's mean."

"Yeah, yeah," Shiloh said as she walked out of Harley's office.

"So what's up?" Harley asked.

"I'm Sydney," the woman said, smiling at Harley shyly.

"Harley," Harley told the girl. "Titles bug me."

The girl chuckled. "I'm working on the program for the logistics division, and… I just can't get past this one part. I was asking around, and everyone tells me that you're, like, programmer extraordinaire… so I thought I'd come ask you."

"Good deal," Harley said.

A discussion ensued about the program, and exactly as Shiloh had expected, they talked programmer-speak the entire time. The young woman left smiling widely. She really liked the new deputy director; the woman was smart.

Kimber received a visitor to her desk later that afternoon. Shiloh leaned on the counter next to where Kimber sat, looking at her pointedly.

"You might want to stay away from Harley," Shiloh said simply.

Kimber took in the other woman's moss-green eyes, sexily streaked hair and pretty face. "Why's that?"

"Because she's very taken, and I don't think you really want to mess with me on this," Shiloh said, her voice low.

Kimber ran a finger over Shiloh's forearm. "I was interested in both of you."

"Well, we're not, so just be smart and leave her alone."

Kimber licked her lips.

"And I'd advise you to stay away from the other new executives too. They're both married and, trust me, you don't want to piss off Shenin's wife. She'll kill you. Stick with Gun," Shiloh said.

"Thanks for the advice," Kimber said, her dark eyes almost glowing with the perceived challenge.

Shiloh shook her head. It would be Kimber's funeral if she tangled with Tyler Hancock—it wouldn't be pretty and it wouldn't end well for the girl. She headed back to her office. Harley had mentioned the conversation with Kimber, and Shiloh had been itching to punch the girl but decided to be a little more diplomatic. She had no problem fighting for her girl, and would do so if necessary.

Later that night, Kimber walked into Jocelyn's office. Jocelyn was working on her computer and glanced over at the girl as she walked in.

"Did you seriously proposition Harley?" Jocelyn asked.

Kimber grinned. "She's hot."

"She's also in a relationship," Jocelyn said, giving the girl a "you should know better" look.

"I know, but it was worth a shot."

"Why?"

"For the fun of it," Kimber said smiling.

"Well, you might want to be smarter about who you flirt with," Jocelyn said.

"Meaning?" Kimber asked, thinking that Jocelyn was acting jealous.

"Meaning if you continue your attempt at getting to all the lesbian executives and make your way anywhere near Shenin Hancock, you're going to come up against a very nasty, very dangerous Air Force security force captain who's not going to bother warning you before she takes you apart."

Kimber stared back at Jocelyn in surprise. Shiloh had said much the same thing. Now she was thinking she really needed to see what this Shenin Hancock looked like.

Jocelyn saw the renewed interest in Kimber's eyes and shook her head. "I won't be able to protect you against Tyler."

"She's tougher than you?"

"I don't know, but that's not what I'm saying," Jocelyn said. "I'm saying I won't."

"You wouldn't try to protect me?" Kimber asked.

"Not if you go after someone that you know is taken, and that you've also been warned not to go near. You don't mess with relationships, Kimber, you just don't."

Kimber shrugged. "You coming over tonight?"

"Uh, no," Jocelyn said. "I'm going to go home and get some real sleep."

"Okay, fine," Kimber said, smiling wistfully.

***

"Are you trying to kill me?" Kashena asked Sebastian as he walked into her office.

"What?" He sat down in front of her desk.

"Did you really tell a member of the press that we're in charge of all law enforcement when there's an emergency?" Kashena asked.

"Well, yeah… but that's true."

"I know it's true, but why the hell would you tell a member of the press that?"

"I don't see the problem here," Sebastian said.

"Baz, just because something's true, doesn't mean you put it right out there."

"What the hell are you talking about?" Sebastian said, looking completely lost.

"You and I know that local law enforcement is under our jurisdiction in an emergency, right?" Kashena said patiently.

"Yeah. Which is what—"

Kashena held up her hand to halt what he was saying. "Do you think they need to hear it from us?"

"I wasn't talking to them," Sebastian said.

"No, you were talking into a huge reservoir of gossip," Kashena said. "And that member of the press has done and reported it. Now, how many phone calls do you think I've gotten about this?" Kashena asked pointedly.

Sebastian squeezed his eyes shut, then opened one eye to look across at his best friend. "A lot?" he asked hesitantly.

"Of course a lot, goddamn it!" Kashena yelled. "You just rubbed their noses in the fact that they are not as autonomous as they think. Jesus, Baz!"

"Okay, okay, I'm sorry," Sebastian said. "I didn't really think about that fact when I said it…"

Kashena shook her head. "You're killin' me, man."

"Did you really tell a member of the press that local law enforcement answer to us?" Gage asked as she walked into Kashena's office, her tone reflecting her chagrin.

"Yes, and I'm already having my balls busted for it, thanks," Sebastian said, giving Kashena a dirty look.

Gage sat down in the chair next to Sebastian, looking tired.

"How many calls have you fielded?" Gage asked Kashena.

"About ten," Kashena said.

"And what are they saying?"

"It's a lot of grumbling," Kashena said. "I can handle it."

Gage smacked Sebastian on the arm. "Be a little more careful next time, will ya?"

"Ma'am, yes, ma'am," Sebastian said.

"Hooah," Gage said, grinning.

"That's an Army thing, right?" Kit said as she walked into the office.

"Yeah," Gage said, laughing. "You ready to go?"

"Whenever you are," Kit said.

Gage held her hand out to Kit. Kit took it, and Gage pulled her down to sit on the arm of the chair. Kit smiled, as did Kashena and Sebastian.

"Heard what happened." Kashena looked at both Kit and Gage, although her look at Gage was pointed. "You did good."

Gage glanced up at Kit. "I did what I needed to."

"Hooah," Sebastian said.

Gage stood, pulling Kit up with her.

"We're going to head out. You two don't stay too late arguing," Gage said, grinning at the two of them.

***

Shenin finished up her paperwork to discharge from the Air Force and walked out of her commander's office feeling just a bit melancholy. Predictably, Tyler was right there waiting for her.

"All civilianized?" Tyler asked as she hugged her wife.

"Yeah…" Shenin said softly.

"Hey, all-new phase, babe," Tyler said.

"Still," Shenin said, moving her shoulders around. "It feels really weird to know I'm never going to put my uniform on again."

Tyler smiled softly. "I get it."

Shenin leaned against Tyler, knowing she was doing the right thing. Taking the job with OES would give her the stability of a job that she could count on to be less stressful. She was still worried about her pregnancy. Because of a badly botched abortion, getting pregnant at all for Shenin had been a miracle. The first trimester had just ended, but she knew the whole pregnancy was risky.

"You with me, babe?" Tyler asked softly.

"Yeah," Shenin answered.

"Come on, let's go home."

Tyler released Shenin but slid her hand down Shenin's arm to hold her hand and lead her out of the administration building. They walked out to Tyler's car, her latest acquisition, a 1970 Chevelle SS in midnight metallic blue. She'd felt the need to get into the classic muscle car competition with the likes of Quinn and Jet. Shenin figured it had to do with the general freak-out Tyler was having over becoming a parent. They both wanted a baby, but for Tyler it was harder as she had the added stress of worrying about Shenin. Hence Shenin had happily indulged Tyler's need for a muscle car.

Tyler started the motor with a deep rumble that had Tyler smiling from ear to ear and Shenin grinning. It was worth every penny to watch Tyler's face light up whenever she drove the car.

"So are you going into the new office tomorrow?" Tyler asked as she drove toward the freeway.

"Yeah, gotta go in and see what I'm working with," Shenin said. "I'm hearing from Gage that the place is a friggin' mess. It's like the previous director was more worried about diddling his secretary than he was in actually directing anyone there."

"Oh, that should be fun," Tyler said, rolling her eyes.

"Ya think?" Shenin asked sarcastically.

"You can do it, babe, you know that."

Shenin smiled over at Tyler. "As long as I have you, I can do anything," she said, her voice soft.

Tyler glanced over at Shenin and took Shenin's hand in hers. Shenin moved over on the bench seat of the Chevelle, snuggling against Tyler. Tyler put her arm around her wife, hugging her close. She turned her head and kissed Shenin's temple.

"You'll always have me, babe," Tyler said.

***

"If you're going to put my girl on that bike, you damned well better be safe, Memphis," Gage said as she watched Kit put the motorcycle helmet on.

"I'll keep her safe, Gage, don't worry," Memphis said, smiling.

"I'll hold you to that," Gage said. "And I don't care if Remi kicks my ass for killing you."

Memphis smiled wider.

Gage leaned in and kissed Kit through the face shield of the helmet she now wore.

"Have fun," she said, pulling back to look into Kit's eyes.

"If Caitlyn starts to drive you crazy, just call me, okay?"

"We'll be fine," Gage said. She smiled. "Grandma Lenna has all kinds of plans for 'girl time.'"

"Oh lord," Kit said, climbing onto Memphis' newly acquired Harley-Davidson Street 750.

The "bois" were going for a ride that day, and Memphis had invited Kit to go with them. Gage was happy to see that the group was taking Kit into their midst, and so wanted to encourage her to hang out with the younger members of the group. Jet and Skyler had more or less started their own club within the group, the Lost Bois.

The Lost Bois also included Cody, Dakota, Talon, Harley, Memphis and now Kit. They often went on rides or cruises in their various cars. This particular trip was a ride up into the mountains. Gage felt a tug at her heart as she watched Kit put her arms around Memphis as Memphis gunned the engine on the bike and pulled away from the house.

Jet sat on her Harley Ultra Limited Low, with Skyler on her recently acquired black-and-red Harley Dyna Street Bob. They both surveyed the group. Cody and Dakota both rode Ninjas—Dakota's was blue and black, Cody's a bright metallic green. Talon drove a Ducati Sport bike in a deep blue. Harley, predictably, rode a Harley-Davidson, a blue Low Rider model. They were waiting for Memphis and Kit in the parking lot of the Griffith Observatory.

"Here she comes," Skyler said as they heard the sound of the 750 burning up the hill.

Memphis pulled into the midst of the group, taking off her helmet and smiling at everyone. Kit did the same, waving to the group.

"'Bout time!" Jet said.

"Gage was being a mother hen," Memphis said.

"Yeah, they're new," Skyler said, referring to Gage and Kit, her light blue-green eyes sparkling humorously,

"Are you saying our girlfriends aren't worried if we kill ourselves?" Talon asked.

"Nah, you and Parker are still newish too," Jet said, laughing.

"So just those of us that have been with our girls for a while aren't cared about?" Cody asked.

"I'm not sure I like that implication," Dakota added with a grin.

"Tough," Skyler said, laughing. "Dev and I have been together longer than all of you, so get over it."

"Okay, so we're headed out to 101, and we'll lead the way," Jet said, smiling as she shook her head at Skyler.

"Just remember not all of us are on a Superleggera," Harley said, her lips curled sardonically.

Jet rolled her eyes. "Blah, blah, blah…"

Cody winked at Skyler. "Sky's slower."

"Fuck you, Cody," Skyler called back.

"That's Kenna's job," Dakota said.

"Uh, I've taken the liberty of updating everyone's iPods," Memphis said, "especially for this ride. The new playlist is called Bangarang, and you can thank Gage for the title track."

Everyone nodded, used to the fact that Memphis frequently shared music on their iPods, sharing her playlists with everyone. It was her way of showing affection for her friends.

"Bangarang," Jet said, grinning.

"Bangarang!" the rest of the group called back.

Everyone put their helmets on and started their iPods in whatever way they listened to music on their bikes. "Bangarang" by techno-rockers Skrillex started, the few words to the song—about being rowdy lost boys—seemed to fit the group pretty well.

It was a two-and-a-half-hour ride through the Angeles National Forest, with lots of winding mountain roads.

Kit had a great time. She found that she did miss Gage, but she knew that Gage was encouraging her to spend time with the group too, wanting her to have their support. She also knew that Gage felt Kit needed to hang out with the younger members of the group to be around people her own age. Kit thought it was silly that Gage thought she was so old, but she found that she really did enjoy hanging out with Memphis and the younger bois. They were a good group.

They stopped at a place called the Grizzly Café, which had an old-log-cabin look to it. People glanced over as they saw the motorcycles pull up. Jet and Skyler grinned at each other as they got off their bikes. They both knew that a bunch of lesbians in the place was likely to shock people. They really didn't care.

Between Harley with her white-blond hair and rainbow braids, Talon with her outrageous and loud personality, and Cody and Dakota bickering like sisters as usual, they were bound to be noticed. Memphis wore her usual level of rainbow paraphernalia, Pride being her top priority. Most of them were fairly butch; even Kit looked more butch than normal since she was wearing riding boots and one of Gage's heavier jackets that had a definite biker style to it.

Inside the restaurant, heads turned as Memphis and Harley debated music, Jet and Skyler talked about the latest surveillance mission they'd done together, and Dakota and Cody debated the pros and cons of Ferrari model years. Talon walked over to Kit, smiling.

"How are you?" Talon asked, having heard about Kit's dramatic rescue by Gage.

"I'm good," Kit said. "Feeling very lucky at this point."

"Sounds like it was a really bad situation," Talon said.

"It was, and Gage kept trying to get me to leave, but... it's just not that easy when you have a child, you know?"

"I can only imagine," Talon said, shaking her head. "But I'm glad you got out okay."

"Thanks." Kit smiled softly. She was having a hard time believing that a world-famous movie star was happy she was okay.

Talon Valois had been in so many movies in the last six years that Kit couldn't even begin to count them all. She'd won a number of Academy Awards, most recently for portraying Jet. Kit had seen the movie, entitled *Jet Blue*, three or four times, loving it as well as the previous movie, *For the Telling*, directed by Legend Azaria, about Legend's own life. Talon had portrayed Legend in that movie and had won an Academy Award for that as well. Talon Valois was very openly gay, and it made Kit proud to know her. The woman was fearless, as were all of the members of the group. Kit knew, without a doubt, that she'd gotten very lucky in becoming part of their group; it still astounded her.

After a very boisterous lunch, the Lost Bois made their way back along a different route to get a new experience. It was a very fun day. Kit arrived back at Lenna's house, flushed but excited about the day.

She walked into the living room and stood watching Caitlyn playing on the floor, Gage sitting right next to her. Gage's back was to her, so she hadn't seen Kit come in. Kit put her finger to her lips to keep Lenna from saying anything.

"So which one is that?" Gage was asking Caitlyn.

"She's Twilight Sparkle," Caitlyn said. "She's purple, see?" She held up the figurine of a purple pony with a mane and tail of dark purple with a pink streak in the middle.

"I see that, yes," Gage said, a smile in her voice. "Which one is your favorite?"

"Pinkie Pie!" Caitlyn exclaimed. "She's pink, see?"

"She's very pretty," Gage said.

"Which one do you like?"

Gage sat back, looking very thoughtful, then she picked up the blue pony with a rainbow mane and tail.

"This one," Gage said, holding up the pony.

"That's Rainbow Dash! She's a troublemaker," Caitlyn said, grinning impishly.

"Well, that sounds about right," Kit said as she walked over to where they sat.

Gage turned around, smiling up at Kit. "Did you have fun?"

"Yes, they are a really cool group," Kit said, her blue eyes sparkling. "And what's going on here?" she asked, looking at all of the toys on the floor.

"Well, Lenna—"

"Nana Lenna," Caitlyn inserted.

Gage smiled. "Apologies. Yes, Nana Lenna decided that Caitlyn's My Little Pony collection needed improving… Hence we now own every My Little Pony in existence."

"Oh my," Kit said, widening her eyes and looking at Lenna. "You didn't need to do that."

"I haven't had a little girl to spoil in over forty years," Lenna said. "I loved doing it."

"And I know you said thank you, right, Caitlyn?" Kit said.

Caitlyn nodded vehemently.

"She did, a few times," Gage confirmed, winking at Caitlyn.

Kit kissed Caitlyn on the cheek. "Good girl. Thank you for being polite."

Caitlyn beamed up at Kit.

Gage looked on, smiling; she enjoyed seeing Kit with her daughter. She very much liked the way that Kit handled Caitlyn, gently and with a great deal of affection. To Gage it said a lot about Kit.

Kit kneeled down and gave Gage a quick kiss. The four of them sat on the floor playing with the My Little Pony collection until dinner time.

"No Gun, huh?" Kit asked Gage.

Gage shook her head. Kit could see it was bothering Gage that Jocelyn had started spending a lot of time away from the house. She knew that Gage was worried about Jocelyn's erratic behavior and that she was spending so much time engaging in days-long sex orgies with two younger women. Kit knew it wasn't jealousy—Gage was worried that Jocelyn's bad-girl behavior was smoke from another fire that Jocelyn wasn't facing, and that was whatever had happened with Sable. Regardless, Gage was keeping her mouth shut, not wanting to alienate her best friend with her worry. Gage knew Jocelyn well enough to know that she'd talk about what had happened when she was ready to do so. Until then, Gage would just sit back and wait.

***

"Just one more shot," Kimber was saying, holding up the bottle of tequila.

"No," Jocelyn said, shaking her head. "I can't even see straight now. You're tryin' to fuckin' kill me."

"No," Donna said, flipping back her dark hair and exposing a very nicely shaped breast. "She's trying to get you so drunk you'll let us do anything we want to you."

Jocelyn narrowed her eyes at Donna, but then started to laugh.

"I don't trust either one of you," she said. "But what exactly is it you think you want to do to me?"

"Mmm," Kimber said with an assessing look. She lay over Jocelyn, pressing her naked body against hers. "I'd start by tying you up…"

"Oh yeah," Donna said, her hand running over Jocelyn's thigh.

"And then I'd love to violate you in every way possible," Kimber said, her eyes sparkling heatedly.

Jocelyn raised one dark eyebrow. "And you think you need to get me drunk for that?"

"No?"

"Nope," Jocelyn said. "When all else fails, try asking."

"Well, we're asking," Kimber said.

"Do your worst." Jocelyn felt so completely numb at that point that her body didn't even seem like her own.

It was another long weekend.

***

After Kit had gotten Caitlyn to sleep that night, she walked into Gage's room. Gage was sitting on the bed, her phone in hand.

"Anything happening?" Kit asked.

"Nothing new," Gage said, setting her phone aside.

Kit walked over to Gage. "You're worried about Gun, aren't you?"

"Yeah," Gage said. "She's running wild right now and heavily overdoing it."

Kit nodded, biting her lip. "Are you in love with her?" she asked, the question that had been circling around in her head for weeks now.

"No," Gage said. "Believe me, I wanted to be, so many times... but I'm not."

Kit sat down on the bed. "Is that why you two aren't a couple?"

"It's part of it, but Gun's the one that sees it clearly. She says I need to be needed, and since she doesn't need me, we can't be a couple."

Kit nodded again. "So the hero thing."

Gage smiled sardonically. "The one thing I really hate to be called."

"But you are," Kit said. "Look at the way you rescued me. You had no thought for your own safety; you just came and got me."

"I told you I'd be here for you."

"But you didn't have to be."

"I wanted to be," Gage said, touching Kit's cheek and leaning in to kiss her.

Kit wrapped her arms around Gage's neck, kissing her back and pressing closer. Gage slid her other arm around Kit's waist and pulled her in the last couple of inches, deepening the kiss. Within minutes they were making love, and Kit did her best to be quiet as she came with Gage's body over hers.

Afterwards they both got up and put a reasonable amount of clothes back on, in case Caitlyn showed up in Gage's room. They weren't sure what Caitlyn thought of things between Gage and Kit, and they'd agreed not to push their relationship onto Caitlyn too quickly.

As she often did, Caitlyn wandered into Gage's room, scrambling up on the bed behind Gage. She sat looking down at her mother lying in Gage's arms, then proceeded to crawl over Gage and lie in the few inches of space between Gage and Kit, turning on her side to face Gage and going back to sleep.

Gage stirred long enough to note what had happened and smile, adjusting to give Caitlyn a little more space. She leaned over to kiss the child on the forehead, then she went back to sleep. Kit woke in the morning and saw what her daughter had done, noting that Caitlyn had her hand on Gage's shoulder. It warmed her heart; Caitlyn had never been that affectionate with Jack, ever.

Gage opened her eyes, looking at Kit over Caitlyn's head.

"I see we had a visitor again," Kit said, smiling softly. "I'm sorry, Gage," she said, thinking that Gage was going to get tired of dealing with a kid all the time. She was probably used to adult relationships that didn't involve kids.

"What are you sorry for?" Gage asked, apparently mystified.

"For this," Kit said, gesturing to her daughter's sleeping form.

"She needs you right now," Gage said. "I get that."

"Uh, she's not lying with her hand on *my* shoulder, Gage. That would be yours," Kit said, grinning.

"Okay, so maybe she needs both of us right now," Gage said.

Kit smiled. "Thank you," she said softly.

"For what?"

"Everything. This, being so sweet to Caitlyn, and me... I just..." Kit shook her head, biting her lip.

Gage propped herself up on her elbow and leaned across Caitlyn to kiss Kit softly. Pulling back, she looked into Kit's eyes.

"You don't have to thank me," Gage said. "I love having you two here with me."

Kit smiled. "I for one love being here," she said, "and I think I can speak for Caitlyn too."

"Good," Gage said, smiling. "Then stay."

"Okay."

***

Jocelyn dragged herself into the house late on Sunday evening. She immediately went into her room, and Gage heard the water running. Determined to talk to Jocelyn, Gage walked into the bathroom.

"Gun?" Gage queried.

"In here," Jocelyn said, sounding exhausted.

Gage walked around the corner and saw Jocelyn sitting in the bathtub full of bubbles, with her knees up and her arms draped over them, her head down. Gage noted a number of hickies and bruises on her neck and back.

"Jesus, Jos… what the hell happened to you?"

Jocelyn laughed hollowly. "Two twenty-somethings and a lot of tequila."

Gage shook her head disapprovingly at her best friend.

Jocelyn glanced up. "Don't fuckin' look at me that way," she growled. "I seem to remember you doing your own share of whoring."

"Yeah, ten years ago," Gage countered snidely.

"So I'm a late bloomer."

"You look like hell."

"Thanks, I love you too," Jocelyn said sarcastically.

"Are you even going to be able to function tomorrow?" Gage asked.

"Yep."

"Okay," Gage said. She knew she wasn't getting anywhere. "I'll leave you alone."

"Goodnight," Jocelyn said dismissively.

Gage left the room. Jocelyn lay back in the tub, hissing as a sharp pain stabbed into her abdomen.

"Jesus, Gun. Less tequila, more judgment," Jocelyn muttered to herself.

She had no idea how many ways Kimber and Donna had used her. She did know that she was literally sore all over and especially in the southern region of her body.

"When all else fails, Gun, just fucking say no," Jocelyn warned herself for next time.

Hopefully she'd remember that, "next time."

Epilogue

It was Friday night, and Kit and Gage were out together for the first time as a couple. Of course everyone had already heard they were a couple now, but the members of the group that were at the Club happily congratulated them.

Jocelyn joined them at the Club that night, having finally pried herself out of Kimber's apartment for a night. Gage was happy to see it for a change. What she was not happy about was the fact that Jocelyn was drinking heavily.

"Get her keys," Jericho told Gage.

"Already have them," Gage said, holding up the keys to the Viper. "I learned how to pick her pocket years ago."

"Smart," Jericho said.

When Cat and Jovina arrived, Jocelyn was outside smoking. Cat walked over to Gage and looked around.

"Where's Gun?" Cat asked.

"Outside smoking, why?" Gage asked, sensing trouble.

Cat simply nodded, then walked toward the patio. Jovina followed her.

Out on the patio, a very drunk Jocelyn was just standing when a pair of hands slid up her chest from behind. Turning, she saw Kimber staring up at her.

"What are you doing here?" Jocelyn asked.

"I thought I'd surprise you," Kimber said, reaching up to kiss her.

"Well, I'm surprised," Jocelyn said, blinking a couple of times.

"That makes two of us," Cat drawled from behind Jocelyn.

Jocelyn turned to Cat, narrowing her eyes a little, then glanced back at Kimber, who was looking at Cat haughtily.

"She's with me," Kimber told Cat.

"She was with someone else about two weeks ago, honey, so don't get comfortable," Cat said. "Where's Sable, Gun?"

"Cat, let's go," Jovina said, pulling at Cat's arm. Cat just shook her head, her eyes on Jocelyn.

Jocelyn stared back at Cat, wavering slightly because the tequila she'd practically been mainlining all night was really catching up to her.

"Last time I heard she was back in London," she said in a bored voice as she shrugged.

"And why is that?" Cat asked, her tone sharpening.

"Like I fuckin' know," Jocelyn snapped.

"So you just tossed her aside and moved on to a ten-year-old?" Cat said snidely, her eyes on Kimber.

"Cat!" Jovina exclaimed, grabbing Cat's arm.

Jocelyn took a couple of steps, getting into Cat's face. "Tell ya what," she said, her voice low. "If you're so fuckin' concerned about Sable, why don't you go to London to take care of her, and I'll take care of your girl while you're gone."

Jocelyn didn't have a chance. Cat punched her in the face, knocking her back.

"Cat!" Jovina screamed, as Jocelyn shook off the punch and rushed Cat, knocking her to the ground and punching her in the face.

The fight was on then, and it took Jericho and Kai to pull Jocelyn off Cat; it also took Quinn and Remington to hold Cat back. Both Cat and Jocelyn were bleeding.

"What the fuck is going on?" Gage yelled as she finally managed to get past the crowd to get to Jocelyn. Her best friend was bleeding from a cut on her lip and from one next to her eye. Gage whirled on Cat. "What the fuck is wrong with you?" she screamed at Cat.

"Me?" Cat exclaimed. "She's the one using women like socks!"

"Yeah, and what do you fuckin' care!" Jocelyn snapped. "You're the one that fucked her over in the first place!" Jocelyn wrenched her arms out of Kai and Jericho's hold, no mean feat, and stalked off.

Gage caught up to Jocelyn outside of the bar.

"What are you doing?" Gage asked Jocelyn.

"She fucking started with me, Jock, not the other way around."

"Okay," Gage said, as Kit walked out of the bar. "Let's just get her home," she said to Kit.

Half an hour later, Gage was helping Jocelyn into bed. Once she had Jocelyn down on the bed, Gage moved to leave. Jocelyn grabbed her arm and pulled her down, fastening her lips to Gage's.

Gage pushed against Jocelyn. Jocelyn pulled her closer.

"Gun, stop!" Gage yelled, shoving away from Jocelyn.

"Fuck..." Jocelyn said. "I'm sorry, Jock... I'm fucked up right now."

"I can see that," Gage said. "What happened with Sable, Gun?"

Jocelyn shook her head. "I don't know."

"What happened?"

"I don't fuckin' know, Jock. Everything was fine, and then she's telling me she's going back to London."

"Okay..." Gage said. "Then what?"

"I asked when she was coming back, and she told me she lives in London."

Gage looked completely shocked. "What the hell?"

"I know, right?" Jocelyn said, blinking slowly as she suddenly got tired.

"Why didn't you just tell Cat that?"

"I don't fucking owe her any explanations," Jocelyn growled.

Gage gazed at Jocelyn for a moment, then nodded slowly. She knew Jocelyn was too proud to tell people about something as personal as what had happened with Sable.

"Are you okay?" Gage asked, looking Jocelyn over.

"Yeah."

"Okay." Gage kissed Jocelyn on the cheek. "I love you, Jos."

"I love you too," Jocelyn replied softly.

Gage left the room then, and Jocelyn turned over onto her side. She gasped as she felt a sharp pain; she needed to learn who not to mess with. She knew she was now at odds with the group, but she also knew that she didn't owe Catalina Roché any explanations. The woman just needed to get over herself.

You can find more information about the author and other books in the *WeHo* series here:
www.sherrylhancock.com
www.facebook.com/SherrylDHancock
www.vulpine-press.com/we-ho

Also by Sherryl D. Hancock:
The *MidKnight Blue* series. Dive into the world of Midnight Chevalier and as we follow her transformation from gang leader to cop from the very beginning.
www.vulpine-press.com/midknight-blue-series

The *Wild Irish Silence* series. Escape into the world of BJ Sparks and discover how he went from the small-town boy to the world-famous rock star.
www.vulpine-press.com/wild-irish-silence-series

CPSIA information can be obtained
at www.ICGtesting.com
Printed in the USA
BVHW031646031120
592326BV00021B/373